VALLEY OF THE SEX DOLLS

SHINGLES, BOOK 38

STEVE WETHERELL

PEGGY'S NEW MOM

P eggy, honey, I want you to say hello to your new mother!"

Peggy Dwight froze on the steps and took in the scene before her in the hallway. Her dad didn't look great, but then he never did these days. His beard had grown long past "passable hipster" and into "unpredictable mountain dweller" some time ago. He seemed to have simultaneously lost weight in his face and gained weight in his gut, making him look both malnourished and morbidly obese at the same time. And his eyes, burdened by heavy baggage at the best of times, seemed a little too wide and alert, almost feral. It was still her dad, Peggy reminded herself, still the same man who tucked her in at night and played cards with her on Sunday evenings, but more and more, in the year since her mom had left, he seemed to resemble a slightly sinister caricature of himself.

All of this she was prepared for. Even him coming home at erratic hours and smelling of what may have been booze or what may have been uncut jet fuel wasn't that uncommon.

The crowbar was new, though. And so was the big, sinister crate. A crate that looked almost like a coffin.

"Dad?" Peggy tried, not knowing where else to start.

"Yuh, honey?" Her dad, Jacob, looked excited. Happy, even. Which was unusual.

"What are you talking about?"

Jacob grinned and gestured to the crate with his crowbar. "Your mom."

Peggy shook her head slowly, wondering if this time her dad had slipped off the deep end completely. "Mom left, Dad. She left a while ago, remember?"

Jacob's eyebrows crashed together like two wiry bison. "No, I don't mean that b… I don't mean her. This is your new mom!"

"Where?"

Jacob turned his palms to the sky and rolled his eyes with the big silly smile he gave her when she pretended not to get one of his deliberately bad jokes. "In the box!"

Peggy looked at the crate. Peggy was just twelve, but she read a lot, and watched a lot, and though she didn't engage much at school, she knew she was sharper than most kids her age. She had heard the phrase "mail-order bride" before but somehow doubted this is what they meant. The dark part of her head, the part of her intellect that toiled away by itself unmindful of the expectations of social norms and the hormonal pressures of a body on the cusp of teenhood, looked for traces of earth on the box and on her father's hands.

Thinking those thoughts irritated her a little, especially when she looked back up to her dad's big, silly, familiar grin. Peggy was quiet in school, with good reason. Sometimes she said stuff that worried other people, even if it was technically true. She didn't really think that her father was responsible for some poor Filipino girl being stuffed into a box and shipped across the ocean, and she didn't really think he'd gone crazy and dug up a body like some dollar-brand Frankenstein. These were unlikely possibilities and uncharitable thoughts. But, still, she was hard pressed to imagine what her dad was actually talking about.

"You're worrying me, Dad."

That was a card she played rarely, and only on justified occasions. It was a shortcut phrase that normally cut through her dad's drunkenness, or his willfully ignorant optimism, or the borderline negligent state of denial he sometimes lived in. It snapped him out of himself. Reminded him that he was the grown-up here, the only grown-up now, and that she, Peggy, for all her careful smarts, was just a little girl. But it didn't seem to work this time.

"Nothing to worry about," he sang. "This is a great day! I'm telling you—all our problems are solved!"

Peggy glanced quickly to the wicker basket by the door where her dad stacked the unpaid bills. The slush-pile was still very much overflowing, and as far as Peggy was concerned, barely being able to make the rent on their modest little home was their only real problem. Her clothes were old, sure, and her smartphone was a good few generations behind her friends, but she was comfortable enough, as long as they had electric and water and a little internet. She folded her arms and raised an eyebrow and hated herself a little for doing it. It was one of Mom's moves.

Jacob nodded, his smile fading a little. "Okay, maybe I should just show you." He wedged the crowbar into the crate and pried the lid off with ease. Then he swept away some packing peanuts and grinned widely. He lifted up what did, indeed, appear to be the body of a woman.

Peggy gasped and felt herself collapse a little on to the step behind her before her rational mind realized what was going on. The woman didn't move like a woman, but like a mannequin. Her dad, strong as he was, probably couldn't lift a real woman up so easily.

So it was a mannequin then. Some kind of sexy mannequin.

Jacob beamed like a proud fisherman holding an unlikely catch. "Peggy, meet Leticia!"

Peggy looked at Leticia. As mannequins went, she was… Peggy thought. "Beautiful" and "realistic" were the words that first came to her head, but they weren't quite the right words. She felt she didn't *have* the right words.

Leticia, whatever she was, was certainly convincing to a point. And she had flawless, tanned skin, made out of something that seemed almost organic. She had wide blue eyes above a full pink mouth. Her hair was a brilliant black, and as thick and long and shiny as any Peggy had ever seen. And her figure, mercifully covered by a plain white slip, was… Well, it was impossible.

That was the flaw, that was what stopped Leticia from being beautiful or realistic. The waist, breasts, butt, and legs were, like her facial features, so exaggeratedly perfect that they didn't quite look right when considered all together. Leticia was beautiful in the same way that Peggy's old Slutz dolls were beautiful, or some of the racier video game avatars on her Game Box. Glamorous, sure, and ticking a lot of boxes of what she herself wouldn't mind in the body department, had she been able to make mother nature a list of demands. But, all together, and without the animus of humanity, Leticia just looked…horrifying.

That was the word Peggy had been scrambling for. Horrifying.

"Well?" Jacob was still grinning hugely.

Peggy's mouth had gone dry. "Well what?"

"What do you think?"

"I don't know, Dad. I don't know what I'm supposed to

think. I guess I'm waiting for a punch line? Or to wake up or something?"

Jacob's cheeks flushed a little. "You're the one who's always telling me to get out and meet some people."

"*People*! People, Dad! Not whatever this is!"

"It's a Real Companion," Jacob mumbled.

"A what?"

"A Real Companion. It's for…those people who don't have an…uh…an adult partner in their lives."

The initial horror that Peggy felt was giving way to a rising conflict of disgust and confusion. "For sex?"

Jacob had the decency to look embarrassed, his free hand rubbing the back of his neck while his other hand wrapped around the Leticia thing's impossibly narrow waist. "Not just for sex," he said. "Not just for that. It's got a computer in it. It can talk a little, say phrases. It's pretty advanced, they reckon it can even adapt to your…um…needs. It's for…it's for lonely people, Peggy, I guess."

Jacob put the doll thing back in the box and slid the lid over. "Look, I knew this was something I couldn't, y'know, sneak around the house. I thought I'd make a little joke about it, but you ain't laughing, so I guess this must have been one of those three-beer plans of mine." He smiled sheepishly.

"Oh really, Dad, just three?" Peggy hated her voice as soon as it came out of her mouth, because it was almost an exact replica of what her mother would have said and how she would have said it, and clearly her dad didn't need that right now.

A silence stretched out between them.

"How much did it cost?" Peggy said, finally.

Jacob perked up again. "That's the beauty of it! It didn't cost me nothing at all, almost. These are an experimental batch. Prototypes. They're going out dirt cheap. I mean, something like this normally costs…well, a shit load more than I can afford, but this was going so cheap I'd be crazy not to get one."

"Crazy. Right."

Peggy didn't quite understand why she was angry at her dad. It wasn't about the money—her dad worked hard at the auto-yard and didn't buy himself anything that wasn't the occasional case of very cheap beer. She suspected the anger would be something she could put into words when she was older and a little wiser. She could see the shape of the outrage, and God knew that was as much as she needed to fly into a sulk these days, but there was something else holding her back. Something that she recognized more easily. She felt sorry for her dad. So sorry it made her want to cry. She knew being embarrassed at your dad was common enough for a teenage girl, and it was easy to get mad about the goofy things he did, especially if they were out in public. But this was different.

"Don't you think this is a little desperate, Dad? I thought you and Darla from the grocery mart were—"

Jacob shook his head. "Honey, you know I ain't into all that. Darla's a fine woman, but she's complicated. Hell, everyone's complicated. I don't want complicated in my life. I just need…" He shrugged and indicated the box. His cheeks flushed even more, and he looked down at his feet.

Peggy was suddenly assaulted by a clear image, an image that usually flashed in her head just before she fell asleep. It was a memory from about a year back, just after Mom had left, a couple of weeks after her affair had been doing the rounds on the gossip chain so much that even Dad, with his blissfully selective world view, couldn't help but hear of it. That night Peggy had crept downstairs for a glass of water and seen her father sitting in front of the television in the dark living room, the sound turned down as it always was, so not to wake her. He had some empty cans of beer at his feet, maybe only a few more than usual. In the flickering blue of the screen, his face was wet.

Peggy had felt a sudden and overwhelming rush of love and warmth then and had been seconds away from diving into his lap and clinging onto his neck and not letting him go until he was all better. But then Jacob had done something that froze her to the spot. He had looked down at his hand, which he then made into a fist, before extending two fingers and a thumb. He tilted his head back and opened his mouth, pushing the fingers into the roof of his mouth before snapping down his thumb. Then he took it out again as though unaware of what he had been doing and stared blankly into the flickering screen once more like nothing had happened.

At that moment, the warmth left Peggy, replaced instead by a ball of ice in her gut. Her dad was a gentle man, who'd never suffer a firearm in the house, even if they did live in the skeeviest area of Oddton Valley. But the implication had been clear. Clear enough that these days she crept down to check on him every time he drank.

"…Be okay?"

Peggy shook her head. Jacob was talking to her.

"What?"

"I said, 'Are you gonna be okay?'"

Peggy swallowed. "I don't know, Dad."

Jacob approached, and put his hand on top of her head like he always did, before running a finger smoothly down her cheek and booping her chin with his thumb. "I know this looks a little weird, but you'd be surprised how common it is now. It's just…it's nothing to be worried about, okay?"

Peggy looked into her dad's wide, sad eyes and nodded her head, slowly.

"Cool," said Jacob. "Now would you give me a hand getting her upstairs?"

"Fuck no, Dad."

"Fair."

***

That night Peggy lay in bed, running the cheap star projector she'd had since she was small. Stars and moons and ringed planets whirled slowly around her dark room, and the sound of the motor whirring was a comfort.

It was one of the last of the childish things she had yet to put away, along with Billy Bear and a stack of picture books she couldn't bring herself to throw out. Most of her small room was bare, but for a desk where she did her homework and played on the third-hand laptop a cousin had passed on to her, and the actually pretty new tablet her dad had bought her as a joint twelfth birthday and sorry-your-mom-ran-out-on-us present.

Other than that, just laundry, books, and a couple of hobby kits she might get around to opening.

It was a lonely room, she supposed. Made a little lonelier on moon-bright nights, when the thin curtain did little to stop the spread of dull silver across the rug. On the desk was a single framed photo of herself, her dad, and her mom. It was taken on a sunny day at one of the annual cookouts they had in Oddton's Henry R. Heyl memorial park. She'd been smaller then, and her dad, sporting a rare almost-clean-shaven chin, picked her up like a suitcase while he lassoed her mom by the waist with his other arm. Her mom looked caught by surprise, her expression somewhere between smiling-at-an-obscure-uncle's-wedding and not-wanting-to-give-a-homeless-person-money. Jacob looked happy, though. He always did in photos.

Peggy was shaken from a doze by the sound of bed springs. The house was small, and the walls thin, and Peggy had seen enough movies and read enough books to counteract Oddton Valley County's stubborn refusal to teach sex education to any child that wasn't already pregnant. In her still muzzy head, she surmised that mom and dad were "At It" again, until she remembered that there was no mom to be "At It" with.

Leticia, she thought, and then shuddered. Thinking of your parents having sex was weird and horrible, even though she knew it was something that every parent did. Her mind recoiled from the thought as though she were equipped by a merciful failsafe. But when she thought of what was happening in the next room, between her father and that expensive hunk of plastic, that mental failsafe didn't operate. Her imagination filled in blanks with terrifying acuity. She folded the pillow around her head, muffling her ears, and stared into the dim of her room with wide eyes. Sleep did not come, but eventually her dad did, and the spring noises stopped.

Peggy waited for what may have been minutes or hours, however long it took for her to relax the grip on her pillow. Her star projector, long in need of a change of batteries, flickered off and whirred to a stop. She sat glumly in the dark before resolving to creep down to the kitchen. There was a little orange juice left in the ice box, and she meant to do something about the bad taste in her mouth.

She swung from her bed onto her nimble feet and crept out of her room. She passed her father's door, slightly ajar, with nothing but opaque black beyond. She paused and held her breath a while, hearing the surprisingly gentle sleep noises of her dad—just slow, steady breathing.

She trod lightly down the stairs, avoiding out of habit the steps she knew to be creaky, and walked into the kitchen, where the light was always left on.

Then she froze.

Leticia was at the kitchen table.

For a while Peggy could do nothing but stare. Leticia was dressed in one of her mom's old robes, which was barely tied around her enormous bosom. The doll thing was sat on the chair, not particularly well posed. Her arms were held out stiffly before her. Her clear, soulless eyes, however, were looking right at the kitchen door. Right at Peggy.

Peggy fought a sudden urge to flee. Why had her dad moved the doll down here? After he had…finished with it? Did he not want it in his bed? Surely there was a better place to keep it when he wasn't…using it.

And, *oh god, did he clean it afterward?*

Peggy's fear was temporarily consumed by her annoyance. She'd talk to her dad tomorrow and draw some lines about what was and wasn't okay about this new situation. She would have to think long and hard about things to put in the "okay" box, and not very long at all about the "not okay" box, but in the meantime, she wasn't going to let some giant dolly stop her moving around her own house.

Peggy held Leticia's gaze defiantly, and then looked away to open the fridge and retrieve the OJ. When she looked back, the carton slipped from her suddenly weak grasp.

Leticia had moved.

Unquestionably. Surely. Maybe?

Had the doll's arms been out straight? They were resting on the table now. Was she remembering properly?

Peggy shook her head and picked up the carton again. She only took her eyes away from the doll for a second and when she looked back…

There was no change. The doll hadn't moved. Leticia's expression remained locked in gasping innocence, her lips parted, her eyes wide. Either Peggy had imagined it, or… Who knew? Didn't Jacob say it had a computer in it? Maybe one of its special functions was to change positions now and then. It didn't matter. It was just a creepy, porny, doll.

Even so, turning her back on it was hard, and going up the dark staircase even harder. No kid liked going up the stairs in the dark, and every kid knew the cardinal rules: you didn't look back because *what if something was there?* And you didn't run because *what if something chased you?*

With a straight back and her head locked into a forward position, Peggy walked calmly up the stairs, careful not to make a sound. She stopped briefly at her father's door to hear the reassuring sound of his breathing, and then walked into her room, and without turning around, slowly shut the door behind her. Then she placed the OJ carton on her desk and climbed quietly into bed, pulling the duvet around her ears so there was only enough room to peek out from. Then she stared at her door handle for an eternity until she fell asleep.

2

SISTERLY ADVICE

The next morning Peggy woke up and tried very hard not to think. She was tired and stressed, and so she gave over completely to her morning autopilot, the ambling ritual of teeth brushing and hair combing unfurling without her consciousness taking any real interest.

It was a school day, and she was always up before her dad anyway, so she didn't have to worry about awkward parental interaction just yet. She flicked her gaze into the kitchen on her way to the front door and noticed with relief that the table was empty of occupants. Then relief gave way to confusion. It wasn't like her dad to wake up once he was out for the night, but she supposed he must have.

Either way, breakfast was the last thing on her mind. She'd grabbed the OJ she'd left on her desk last night, and that would have to do her until lunch.

If the brisk air of a surprisingly cool Midwest morning didn't clear her head, then the sonic hammer of the school bus certainly did, and Peggy was feeling more or less awake by the time she walked through the chain-link gates of

Oddton Valley Junior High. She spotted Josh McKenzie almost immediately, sat against a wall on his backpack with his smartphone in his hand as usual. Josh liked to maximize every free second by watching the myriad MyTube stars he followed and stuffing as much of their daily babble into his head as he could. He looked up with a familiarly resentful expression as Peggy stood over him.

"Oh hey, Peggy, you look like shit," he said, casually.

"So do you," Peggy replied. She meant it too. It wasn't just the standard insult exchanging that punctuated most of their interactions—Josh's eyes were more glazed and red-rimmed even than usual.

"Yeah," he said. "I didn't sleep much last night. My mom and dad were really going at it."

"Oh, gross, Josh."

Josh snorted. "Not like that. I mean they were arguing."

"What about?"

Josh shook his head slowly. "You wouldn't believe me if I told you."

Before Peggy could reply, Marsha walked over, her presence and poise demanding immediate attention as usual. "You guys are not gonna believe this…"

Peggy smiled politely. Marsha was the Popular Girl. Not just because she was an early developer, loud, pretty, and rich by Oddton standards, but because she just decided she was one day and everyone seemed to be going along with it just fine. Peggy kind of liked her. Marsha wasn't like the alpha girls in the movies and teen dramas. She was vapid, yes, but actually kind of sweet. Marsha's idea of being Miss Popular seemed to consist of getting as many people to like her as possible. Hence her daily rotation of gossip magazine chitchat would routinely include even the withdrawn Peggy and the mostly oblivious Josh.

Marsha opened her mouth, and in a single breath, said,

"Do you remember how I told you my dad wouldn't buy me the Corporate Cathy limited edition Power Spa and Board Room combination play set for my eleventh birthday because it was a big expense and he already got me the custom Audi TT that transforms into a nail bar?"

Peggy exchanged a look with Josh. Marsha was such a raw force of nature when it came to the pleasantly mundane that it was difficult to keep track of exactly what first-world problem was currently bothering her. She was like a hurricane of harmless bullshit.

"Uh…sure, Marsha, we remember that," Josh said, unconvincingly.

"Well, you'll never guess…" Marsha continued. "You'll never guess what he comes home with last night."

Peggy and Josh nodded in simultaneous agreement. They would never guess.

"He comes home with a full-sized dolly. I mean, this thing must have been way expensive. It probably cost more than, like, a hundred Corporate Cathys. And you know what? It wasn't even for me! He says I can't have one until I'm older. I mean, don't get me wrong, I'm super over Corporate Cathy, what am I, like, a six-year-old? But still—"

"Wait," Josh interrupted. "Your dad bought a doll? Like a grown-up sized doll? Kind of looks like someone stuffed a Kardashian with Jell-O?"

Marsha put a finger to her lips. "I kind of thought it looked like someone put Cardi B in a condom and squeezed her real hard in the middle."

"My dad got one too…" Peggy heard the words before she realized she was speaking. "Last night he…uh…unboxed it. They're called Real Companions, right?"

Marsha shrugged. "My dad said its name was Crystalle, but sure."

Josh nodded slowly. "Same deal here. My dad came home with one last night."

Peggy blinked. She knew Marsha's dad was single, but Josh's parents were definitely still together. "What did your mom say?"

"She hit the fucking roof!" Josh said. "That's what they were arguing about last night."

"I think I can see where she's coming from," Peggy offered, tentatively.

"Well, duh," Josh sighed. "Not my dad, though. He said my mom burns through magic wands like the Battle of Hogwarts, so why shouldn't he get a toy?"

Marsha made a face. "I don't know what any of that means, but I think it might be gross." She turned and left.

Josh squinted after Marsha. "Do you think she knows what the dolls are? What they're for?"

"I'm not even sure that *I* know what they're for," said Peggy. "Not really."

Josh looked down at his screen. "They're for...y'know... jerking off with, right?"

"I was going to say having sex with."

"Same difference." Josh shrugged. The school buzzer rang, and Josh flipped his phone into his pocket and left. Peggy stood alone for a while, waiting for the sudden surge of inexplicable annoyance to fade before she went inside. She didn't know how to explain it to Josh, or even to herself, but she didn't think those two things were the same at all.

***

The school day came and went as it usually did. Peggy thought of her school days like an elastic band—they stretched out, full of tension and potential pain, and then the final buzzer sounded and they snapped instantaneously back into a wiggly mess that you put in your pocket and forgot about.

The weather had picked up, and Peggy was in no hurry to get home anyway, so she decided to walk home via the mini-mall and see if she could spend the handful of dollar bills she kept scrunched up in her backpack pocket for just such an occasion. The mini-mall didn't have a lot going for it. An *OK Shopping!* a liquor store, a long-abandoned Hello Kitty Sex Emporium. The rest was mostly dry cleaners and takeout food places. It was only slightly less boring than the rest of Oddton, unless you went there after dark, when it became *really* exciting, providing your idea of excitement was getting stabbed by meth addicts.

But, better still than the prospect of comic books and candy was that Typhoon Mary would be there.

Mary was a friend of sorts. By night she was a stripper at the Dollar Bill Club and lived in the Sweaty Palms Motel across the street from the mini-mall. Mary spent her days standing outside the liquor store and "networking" as she put it, which seemed to consist entirely of smoking cigarettes and handing out business cards to hunted-looking men.

Mary was an unlikely friend, but Oddton Valley was a small place, and when Peggy's mom had left, Mary was one of the few people who stopped her in the street and told her how sorry she was, and to keep her chin up, and did she want a cigarette, maybe? Peggy had declined the cigarette, of course, but since then they'd always chatted amicably, and with Mary being one of the few adult women in her life that wasn't a teacher, Peggy had come to enjoy their interactions.

Peggy had never asked how Mary knew who she was or found out that her mom had left, but she suspected that her dad wouldn't have been the first man to sigh his problems into a stripper's cleavage and probably wouldn't be the last.

Peggy also never asked why Mary was called Typhoon

Mary. She felt that she could probably puzzle it together, but instinctively knew that doing so was a bad idea.

"Hey, kid!"

Peggy looked up. Mary was there all right. She was currently riding on a coin-operated pony ride outside of the Eat N' Leave. She was dressed in her usual—a pair of PVC shorts that disappeared into her butt crack like they were vacuum sealed, and a high cut tank top that covered just enough of her boobs that she wouldn't get arrested. She waved with one hand and held a half-sucked popsicle to her mouth with the other. She gripped the cartoony horse beneath her with bare thighs that were accustomed to the much more arduous task of holding her weight while she spun around a pole at high speeds.

Peggy wondered why she was riding the inanely grinning pink horse, but then she noticed a man walk by, become transfixed by the slow smooth rocking of Mary's hips, and walk directly into a trashcan. Mary threw a business card his way with practiced ease. He pocketed it and walked hurriedly away with his head down. This was more "networking," Peggy surmised.

"Hi!" Mary elegantly dismounted the horse and sucked the remainder of the popsicle down her throat in a way that would have made a close-up magician scratch his head. Another man walked into the same trashcan.

"Hey, Mary," said Peggy. "How's tricks today?"

Mary lit a cigarette and scowled. It was difficult to tell how old Mary was under the wig and make-up. She could have been a severely overworked twenty-five-year-old or a forty-year-old in really good shape. "Slow, kid," she said. "Last night we had one customer at the Dollar Bill Club. That's unheard of, even for a school night. Ever seen seven exotic dancers fighting for a lap dance with one customer? That guy's lucky to be alive…"

"Not a good night, huh?"

Mary shook her head. "That's why I'm dispensing with my usual level of subtlety today. Need to drum up some business. I've got my 401K to think of."

"Gotta hustle, right?" Peggy grinned.

Mary tipped a wink. "That's right, kid. Work hard, make your own money, don't be in debt to no one. It's the only way a girl can get ahead in life." Mary opened her tiny purse and pulled out a Chonkachew bar. She looked at Peggy and raised an eyebrow before snapping it in half and offering a piece to her.

Peggy smiled and took the sticky chocolate, cramming it entirely into her mouth. The two women stood a while, cheeks full of chocolate gunk, jaws working up and down furiously. Mary crossed her eyes. Peggy wiggled her eyebrows. Mary straightened her back and threw a military salute. Peggy began to tap dance. Mary's eyes widened and she doubled over, spitting out chocolate goop onto the pavement as she laughed hysterically.

"You win again, kid," she said, after a while.

Peggy spoke through a mouthful of delicious goop. "Don mesh withda besht."

Mary wiped her mouth. "Not like I need the calories anyway. So, how're things at home?"

Peggy nodded her head while she finished chewing and swallowing. "Not great. My dad is... I don't know. I don't think he's doing too well."

"Oh?" Mary squatted down until she was level with Peggy. "You know you can talk to me about anything right? Us girls, we stick together."

Peggy felt herself blush. "It's a little weird. I'm not sure if I can explain it."

"Try me."

Peggy tried to line up her thoughts, feeling the tension in

her tummy rising up in anticipation of the sweet release of sharing, but then something behind Mary caught her eye. "Leticia?" she gasped.

Mary frowned and turned around, her eyes widening. "What the shit is that?"

Peggy's mouth gaped. She could have sworn it was Leticia, somehow floating along next to an old man in a tracksuit. But then she noticed little differences. Lighter hair, paler skin, bigger boobs. It was a Real Companion alright, but not her dad's. And, astonishingly, it seemed to be moving by itself.

"What the fuck is this, Arno?" Mary snapped.

The old man in a tracksuit looked up with feigned astonishment. He was an oily-looking guy, missing a fair few teeth, with what was left of his suspiciously black hair plastered to his scalp with what might have been cheap product, or some naturally occurring grease. "Why, Mary doll, I didn't see you there!"

"Oh really?" Mary put her hands on her hips. "That's what you said when I caught you jerking off outside my motel window."

Arno shrugged his skinny shoulders. "What harm is there in an old man tending his private business? So what if I happened to be in the vicinity of your window?"

"No harm at all as long as you're paying me," Mary snapped. "Now answer my question—what the fuck is this?" She leveled a well-manicured finger at the Real Companion.

Arno grinned, wetly. "This is my woman. This is Lucille."

"Lucille, huh?"

Peggy peered around Mary's broad hips. She noted that "Lucille" was in roller boots, and the old man, Arno, was pulling her along on what looked like a dog lead.

Mary walked around the doll. "So, this is the next step

down from being a peeping tom, is it? Fucking Barbie's trailer trash cousin?"

"Don't you talk about Lucille like that!" Arno snapped. "She's good to me. She takes care of my needs."

Mary arched an eyebrow. "Oh really? Even those *special* needs of yours?"

Arno's grin turned sly. "Ain't nothing you can do that Lucille can't do better."

"Oh really?" Mary stepped forward, slowly, pinning Arno with her cool gaze. "Does she call you Big Dog?"

Arno snapped his fingers. Peggy jumped as the Real Companion suddenly straightened and tilted its head. It spoke in a toneless voice, not moving its lips. "I love you, Big Dog."

Mary staggered back in shock.

"And she doesn't even charge me extra," Arno chuckled.

Mary shook her head, at a loss for a retort.

"Come, Lucille," Arno sniffed. He tugged on the doll's leash, sending her rolling behind him. "Let's not dally any more with these low women."

Mary watched them go in quiet fury. "What the hell even was that?" she growled.

"They're called Real Companions," Peggy said. "My dad got one, too."

The anger faded from Mary's eyes, replaced by something else, something sadder. "Your dad has one?"

Peggy shrugged apologetically. "A lot of people do now."

"A lot...?" Mary stepped back, her weight collapsing suddenly onto the wall behind her. "Those fuckers," she said, faintly. "They can't stand for us to have even one thing over them, those fuckers."

Peggy was unsure what to say, suddenly regretting opening her mouth in the first place. "I bet they don't dance real good, though, right?" she tried.

Mary snorted a laugh. "Dancing's just what primes the pump, kid, and a man don't need priming is someone's already sucked the water out of his tap."

"What?"

Mary shook her head, as though suddenly remembering who she was talking to. "Nothing, sweetheart. I'm going to call it a day. I'll see you around, okay?"

"Okay."

Peggy watched Mary leave. In all the months of their friendship, Peggy had never seen the woman look so defeated.

3

FAMILY

The sun was starting to set when Peggy finally reached her street. The identical little houses lined up on the cracked pavement and squinted with dark windows into the harsh orange light. She could already hear the whoops and crashes and peeling wheels of those preparing for dark. After the day she'd had, Peggy was looking forward to nothing more than curling up on her bed with a book and her tablet. She hoped her dad had bought some snacks.

She sighed through the front door, dumped her backpack in its usual spot, and went immediately to the kitchen. The sight that greeted her was nearly, *so nearly*, idyllic. Her dad was cooking. He rarely did. Sure, he heated something up every night, but actually standing there with a kitchen towel over his shoulder, neatly chopping vegetables, with a couple of pots already on the boil? Not since Thanksgiving had she seen him so domestically engaged. He was even singing some old Frank Sinatra tune. Peggy's smile never quite made it to her eyes though, because waiting at the kitchen table was Leticia.

The table was dressed, cutlery and place mats laid out, and a couple of candles burning for show. Leticia, it seemed, had also made an effort—wearing one of Peggy's mom's few "going out" dresses and silver earrings. Her dad had even gone so far to gather the doll's hair up in a surprisingly elegant bun. Not bad for a guy who had once sent her to school with two pigtails on the same side of her head.

"Oh, hey honey!" Jacob smiled. "I thought I'd cook us dinner tonight."

Peggy tried to keep a lid on the bubbling emotions rising in her gut. "What's the occasion?" she said.

"Oh, no occasion," Jacob sang, merrily. "I just thought it'd be nice to make a little effort."

"You're sure?" Peggy said, coolly. "You're sure it's not because we have a guest?"

Jacob froze in his ministrations for a moment, before carrying on as though he hadn't. "You mean Leticia? Ha! Yeah, I thought it'd be funny, you know?"

"It's not, though, Dad. It's not funny at all."

Jacob shrugged, and carried on chopping. "Yeah, well, you know. We're having dinner anyway, so what harm does it do? It's nice to have the company. Makes a change from just the two of us."

"Okay, yeah, you want me to go and get Billy Bear? I think I still have an old GI Jake lying around. Should we set a place for Sargent Killtime?"

Jacob snorted a quiet laugh. "That ain't the same thing, honey."

Peggy tried to shut her mouth, but the anger wouldn't let her. "Yes, it is, Dad. It's exactly the same thing. Billy Bear is exactly as real as Leticia. Or do I have to shove a flesh-light inside him, first?"

Jacob chopped in silence for a while, the blade moving slowly, without rhythm. He cleared his throat. "Look, I just want us all to sit down and have a nice dinner together like a—"

Peggy stamped her foot. "I will not sit and eat next to that...that *thing!*"

Suddenly the chopping board was on the floor, Jacob's thumping fist sending carrots and broccoli flying. "*You will not talk that way about your mother!*" he roared.

Peggy staggered back, looking from the unfamiliar rage on her father's face to the glassy-eyed impassiveness of the doll thing. "Dad, you're worrying me," she said.

Jacob looked down at his shoes, shoulders heaving up and down. "I just had a long day," he said. "I didn't sleep well, I..." He began to pick up the scattered vegetables. "I can clean these off, they'll be okay, I'll boil them good. I'll fix you something and bring it up to your room for you."

Peggy swallowed hard against the tears and nodded. She supposed she had been sent to her room, but that was where she was going to go anyway. She didn't want to even be on the same floor as the doll.

Once she reached her bed, what was left of her resolve cracked, and the tears came fat and heavy. She put a pillow over her head so her dad wouldn't hear her, and then she wrapped the duvet around herself and, without really meaning to, fell asleep.

When Peggy awoke, the lights in her room had been turned out. She lay in soft confusion for a while, her eyes adjusting to the bright moonlight phasing through the curtains. On her desk was her dinner and a glass of water. How long had it been there? She was in her t-shirt and underwear, and she realized with some embarrassment that her dad must have taken her jeans off without even waking her. Had she been so tired?

Her stomach growled, and the prospect of a meal, however cold it now was, jockeyed for position over the desire to stay in her warm bed. She sat up, her eyes puffy, feeling the soothing lightness in her chest that a good cry will bring.

She blinked, hard, clearing her eyes, and stared wide eyed into her room.

When she saw Leticia, sitting on her desk chair by the bedroom door, she didn't feel fear at first. She felt, instead, a sense of unreality, suddenly sure she was dreaming. The doll was back in its nightgown, sitting with its legs crossed daintily, hands on its knee, staring right at her.

"This is my room," Peggy whispered. "This is my room and you're not supposed to be in here."

A toneless voice rang out, causing Peggy to jump.

"Be a good girl," the doll thing said, its lips not moving. "Be a good girl."

Peggy's flesh crawled, and she thought she might slip into panic then, but she was premature in her terror. What happened next was far more awful, far more dreadful. Leticia stood up. She did not stand like a human, with the careful unfolding of limbs, the familiar gravity. She moved without weight, and without logic, as though by a bad stop motion animator with no regard for anatomy. Then the doll turned in utter silence and strode from the room on feet as light as feathers, leaving Peggy alone in the dark.

There was only a beat of silence before the shriek forced its way out of Peggy's throat, and once she started, she couldn't stop. An electric chill grasped her body, and horrible panic numbed her mind utterly. She wasn't sure how long she screamed, but the light flicked on and her dad stumbled in, squinting, his beer gut hanging over his tatty pajama bottoms. He gathered her up like fallen leaves, holding her together.

"Oh, my girl, my girl, what's wrong? What's wrong, girl?"

Peggy pushed her face into the warmth of her dad, unable to remember when she'd last felt so small, so vulnerable. "It was her, Dad! She was in my room!"

"Who?"

"Leticia!" Peggy pushed herself away so she could look her father in the eye. "That doll was in my room! It spoke! It...it moved!"

Jacob's eyes flickered as they searched her face. "Honey, that's impossible. You must have had a nightmare."

Peggy sniffed and shook her head. "No. She was here. It was real as day. Daddy, I want her gone, I want her out of here, please! She scares me!"

"Oh, honey." Jacob enveloped her again. "I...I know this must seem strange to you."

Peggy sobbed an unintelligible reply.

"But, you have to listen. I...I can't just throw her out."

"Why not?"

"It was part of the contract, honey. I told you I got her for cheap, right? This is beta testing, and I'm kind of...well, legally obligated to see through the trial period. I signed a contract."

Peggy looked at her dad's mournful face and could not bring a reply that wasn't more tears.

"I'm so sorry," Jacob said. "I never would have done this if I'd known you'd feel this way. I don't know what I was thinking. It just...it just all seemed to make sense at the time."

"I don't want to see her anymore, Dad, please!"

Jacob nodded with some resolve. "I'll tell you what. From now on she doesn't leave my room, okay? Hell, I'll even put a padlock on so that when I ain't in there, no one else can get in there, alright? You won't have to see her anymore. And as soon as the trial's done, I'll give her back and it'll just be you and me again, okay?"

Peggy nodded slowly. "I guess."

"It's gonna be okay, honey. You'll see."

"Dad?"

"Yes, sweetheart?"

"Will you stay in my room tonight?"

Jacob sighed and smiled and nodded his head. He pulled the chair over from the door and leaned it against the bed. Then he tucked Peggy in and sat with his arms folded over his hairy chest. "Just you go to sleep. I'll be right here."

Peggy nodded, and, when her sniveling hiccups eventually subsided, she was soon fast asleep again.

———

She did not know what time she woke up in the night, but her dad was gone and she heard the steady creaking of bed springs.

———

By the time Peggy got to school the next day, her sadness and fright had been numbed by exhaustion. She had woken up unsure if the incident with the doll had just been a dream or some kind of hallucination. She had been very sick once, a bad flu, and had seen all kinds of crazy things, but this hadn't felt like that. It had been as real as anything, except that it couldn't have been.

"You look like shit," said Josh.

Peggy looked up and blinked, realizing her feet had taken her halfway into the school building.

"Your mom looks like shit," she retorted without thinking.

"Actually, you're right." Josh yawned. "Dad made her sleep on the couch last night. You would not believe how much she couldn't shut up about her neck hurting. I was like, 'Bitch, I don't care about your neck, get me my Cheerios and leave me out of your drama.'"

"You said that to her?"

"Hell no," said Josh. "My head is still attached to my body, ain't it?"

Peggy blinked as certain words dallying in her ears finally plopped into her mind. "Your dad made your mom sleep on the couch?"

"Well, yeah, the bed's only big enough for him and Crystalle. Come on, we're gonna be late."

Peggy followed Josh's lead and increased her pace. Nobody wanted to be late for Ms. Shipman's class. She was one of those teachers who had very little else in her life but the power she had over the children in her charge. And boy did she get a kick out of using it.

Surprisingly, when they burst through the classroom door, Ms. Shipman wasn't there. The rest of the students were lined up at their desks in neat rows, staring ahead with the flat anticipation of boredom at the empty board. Peggy exchanged a facial shrug with Josh and they each went to their desks.

Somebody shuffled loudly in their seat. Peggy judged there was perhaps a few seconds before the realization that Ms. Shipman wasn't coming in today hit their collective psyches and the standard chaos of unsupervised children was unleashed. Before that could happen, though, Principal Mathews entered, kicking the door open and backing up with all the grace and efficiency his ovoid shape would allow him. He was wheeling something behind him, an office chair with a woman sat in it.

No, Peggy realized. Not a woman. Another Real

Companion. This one sporting a ginger beehive and a pair of cat style spectacles. Her ludicrous tits were barely buttoned into a sensible white shirt, and her thick, white thighs all but made redundant a too-tight black pencil skirt.

"Good morning, class!" said Principal Mathews.

The class muttered various iterations of noncommittal noises.

Mathews finished wheeling the chair behind the desk. Then he took an apple from his pocket, buffed it on his suit Eltonet, and placed it carefully before the glassy, green-eyed gaze of the doll. He then looked down with the obvious satisfaction of someone acknowledging a job well done. Then he continued to look, and Peggy realized with alarm that the front of his suit pants was beginning to fill out.

"Um…Principal Mathews?" someone said.

The principal shook himself from his internal musings and noticed the class again. "Ah, yes, I was saying… This is Ms. Firm, she'll be stepping in for Ms. Shipman from now on. I expect you treat her with the same respect you'd treat any substitute teacher…" Principal Mathews thought about what he'd just said. "I expect you to treat her with respect," he amended. "Now, behave." The principal ran a finger lightly across the Ms. Firm doll's shoulder and cast longing gazes back at her as he left the classroom.

There was silence. Peggy felt like she could hear her nerve endings.

Someone behind her cleared her throat. Peggy thought it was Marsha. "What is going on h—"

"Quiet, please."

The class gasped. Ms. Firm's head had tilted only a little, and her mouth hadn't moved from its "insert penis here" position, but the toneless voice had carried throughout the classroom with strange authority.

Peggy shuddered. Hearing the thing's voice had brought

back her nightmare full force. If it had indeed been a nightmare.

Ms. Firm looked straight ahead again, her lifeless eyes focusing on nothing Peggy could discern. "Please open your biology textbooks at page fifty-three," the doll said.

There was the noise of twenty or so kids retrieving their books as carefully as possible and flipping them to the correct page.

Marsha snorted. "This is crazy," she said. "This is a doll, not a teacher. We can't just—"

"Will you shut up?"

Peggy turned with some shock to Josh. She didn't think she'd ever heard him snap like that at anyone, and least of all at Marsha, who was basically a well-dressed puppy. "Can't you see she's trying to teach?" he added.

"Yeah." This time it was Mack Johnson, the class tough guy, a boy who had once kicked a teacher straight in the balls after an inquiry about late homework. "Some of us are here to learn," he grumbled. Both Josh and Mack turned back in their seats, giving their full, unwavering attention to Ms. Firm.

Peggy looked around. It wasn't just Mack and Josh. All the boys were looking at the Real Companion with the same devoted attention they usually reserved for sniping their friends in the head on *War is Duty Online*.

The girls were quiet too, but it was a unique kind of quiet. The kind of quiet kids had when someone was getting chewed out, and they didn't want to be next. They shot each other worried glances. The air was loaded with tension, and thick with unease.

Ms. Firm began reciting page fifty-three apparently not needing a textbook of her own to reference. She spoke like a text-to-speak program, Peggy realized. Had Principal

Mathews somehow programmed her with an entire lesson? An entire curriculum? Would she be here all term?

Peggy hoped not, because she felt there was a very real chance that after a couple of days of this, she might lose her fucking mind.

A t lunchtime Peggy lined up for tater tots, shuffling along the queue like a very polite zombie. With her tray loaded, she scanned the hall until she saw Josh sitting at a table by himself, chomping on a tuna-fish sandwich in that particularly indifferent way people who eat tuna-fish sandwiches have.

She sat down opposite him and narrowed her eyes until he looked up.

"What?" he said, blinking in puzzlement.

"Seemed like you were really interested in biology today," Peggy said.

"Yuh," said Josh. "So?"

"So, since when are you into science?"

Josh rolled his eyes as he chewed the last of his sandwich. "I'm not 'into science.' The only people who say they are 'into science' are people on the internet who think factoids are the same as learning. I just…you know, biology is important, so I want to do well in it."

Peggy didn't break eye contact. "Didn't you always say you were going to go into law, like your dad?"

Josh shrugged. "Maybe I'll be a renaissance man. Biologist by day, lawyer by night."

"So your sudden interest in biology has nothing to do with Ms. Firm's big plastic boobies?"

Josh slapped his hand on the table. "They're not plastic.

They're a polyglycerol blend over collagen scaffolding covering twin self-heating silica packs."

Peggy stared at Josh, wordlessly.

Josh blushed, darkly. "That is, I think I read that somewhere."

"So," Peggy began, "you know she's not real, right?"

"Of course I know that!"

"So when I saw you doodle 'Josh loves Ms. Firm 4 eva' in your notebook just now, that was…what?"

Josh scrambled the notebook he clearly hadn't realized he was still scribbling hearts in under the table. "Give me a break, would ya? I just think she's pretty, is all."

At that moment Marsha came by with her own tray. "Hi there," she said.

It took a little second for Peggy to wonder what was off about Marsha, but then she realized all the myriad little changes that, impressively, the girl had managed to implement in the few minutes between class and lunch. Her hair was up in a beehive, and she'd found a new shade of red lip gloss. Her shirt, a simple button up, had been modified with safety pins until it appeared two sizes two small. More noticeably, it seemed Marsha's boobs had grown by more than a couple of cup sizes, thanks to some expert bra padding. She had even managed to find a pair of cat-style spectacles from somewhere, despite her always wearing contacts before now.

Incredulous amusement was only briefly Peggy's response, before it was taken over by something a little older and sadder. Nice or not, Marsha was the popular kid, and you didn't stay the popular kid without knowing which way the wind was blowing. Marsha was on board with the latest trinket trends even before the MyTube influencers, and knew what the latest look was going to be way before it reached normal high-street stores. She had a knack for it.

Peggy realized she wasn't looking at her friend playing dress up. She was looking at the future.

Josh seemed to realize this too, she thought. He smiled at Marsha in an entirely unfamiliar way. "Sup?" he said, in a very un-Josh-like manner.

Marsha smiled and tilted her head demurely. Again, a mannerism that Peggy had never seen her deploy before.

"Josh and I were just talking," Peggy began, carefully, "about how silly it is to have a crush on someone who isn't real."

Marsha blinked, innocently. "Oh, you mean like an anime character or something?"

"She means Ms. Firm," Josh said.

"I don't think that's silly at all," Marsha said. "I think Ms. Firm is very pretty."

"But she isn't real!" Peggy snapped, louder than she'd intended. "She's just some cartoon character of a woman. Something designed purely to give horny old men boners!"

Marsha sniffed and averted her eyes. "Sounds like someone's jealous."

"Jealous!" Peggy felt her cheeks flush. "How could I possibly be jealous of a…of a thing?"

Even as she said the words, she knew it wasn't quite true. She was old enough to know that jealously was perhaps the least rational of emotions. She suspected people got jealous about things all the time. Was she jealous of Ms. Firm? Was she jealous of Leticia? The strange internal question blindsided her with confusing new emotions, which, like most confusing new emotions in a twelve-year-old girl's brain, quickly transmogrified into inexplicable tears.

"You seem pretty jealous to me," Josh said, quietly.

Peggy got up without a word, leaving her lunch behind her. Then she hurried to the nearest bathroom where she could hate herself for crying in peace.

4

UNDER THE HOOD

After school, Peggy once again strolled to the mall, her footsteps as heavy as her heart. When she arrived, she found it to be strangely quiet. Typhoon Mary was there, exhibiting none of her usual hustle. She leaned against a wall, smoking a cigarette and staring dead eyed at the horizon.

"Hey, shug," she mumbled, not bothering to put her cigarette out like she usually did when Peggy came close.

"Where is everyone?" said Peggy.

Mary shrugged. "Hell if I know. Place is a ghost town." Mary forced a smile. "Why the long face?"

Peggy told her. Not about Marsha padding her bra, or Josh making her feel so weirdly angry, but about Ms. Firm, their new substitute teacher.

Mary listened, her half-hearted smile fading from her face with her every word. "One of those things is teaching kids now? That's insane."

"Right?"

Mary threw her cigarette to the floor and stamped on it vengefully. "You know what women need? A fucking labor union. Homemaker or surgeon, doesn't matter, you got tits, you're in. Christ."

Peggy finally gave voice to a rising suspicion. "Do you think they're trying to replace us?"

Mary looked into Peggy's eyes and seemed to notice something that softened her expression. "Listen, shug. I've known a lot of guys and I can tell you something that's true for all of them—there's usually a solid six-inch gap and a whole lot of hormones between what they think they want and what they actually want. No. I don't think they're trying to replace us. They're not that dumb."

Peggy shrugged. "I think my dad's definitely trying to replace my mom."

Mary tapped her foot. "How is your dad? How's his new…thing?"

"He seems…" Peggy searched for the right word. "Happy and guilty?"

"Yeah, I get it." Mary tapped a well-manicured finger on her glossy lips for a moment. "The Germans probably have a word for that. Hey, maybe we should check in on your dad?"

"What? You and me?"

"Yeah, sure."

Peggy's subconscious searched her social development files for the correct etiquette for bringing a stripper home. She came up with a resounding blank. "Won't that be unusual?"

"Nah." Mary waved a hand dismissively. "Me and your dad are cool."

"You…uh…know each other? From work?" Peggy held her breath.

Mary looked down at her and there was that sudden reshuffling of features that happened when Mary remembered who she was talking to. Peggy supposed that she didn't spend a lot of time around kids. "Your dad drops by the club now and then." Mary sighed. "He watches me dancing, and sometimes he'll buy me a beer and we'll chit chat. But Jacob's a perfect gentleman. Or as much as anyone can be a perfect gentleman in a strip joint, I guess."

"So, you're like…work friends?"

"That's typically what dudes tell their wives, sure. If it makes you feel any better, you know your dad and I used to go to school together, right?"

Peggy shook her head. She did not know that.

"Sure! We both went to Oddton. There were a couple of years between us, and we never really mixed in the same circles, though. Your dad was a jock. I mean, he was the worst linebacker on the team, but he was still *on the team.* Everybody loved him. Guy was a hoot."

"He was?" Peggy tried to envision her dad younger, thinner, and without the perennial look of mild hurt in his eyes, and found that she couldn't, really. "I didn't know that."

"So, do you think he'd mind an old school friend dropping by? Rather than some ho?" Mary grinned.

Peggy felt her cheeks flush. "I didn't mean it like that."

"I know, sweetheart, I'm just playing with you. Now, let's go get my car."

"It's not far to walk," Peggy protested.

"Yeah, but my tools are in my car," said Mary. "And I think it's high time we learned what makes our new dolly friends tick."

Peggy stared at Mary in puzzlement. The stripper grinned. "Oh, your dad was a jock, sweetie, but I was all about science club."

Evening was fading in as Mary's car rolled up outside of Peggy's home. Peggy had to admit she was a little disappointed. If someone had asked her what kind of car Typhoon Mary drove, she would have guessed something pink, and classic, with maybe a fun graphic or sassy bumper sticker. The compact, gray Honda was about as far away from that fantasy as possible. ("It gets great mileage, though," Mary had said. "And the guy practically paid me to take it off his hands. All because it needed a new carburetor, like *that's* hard to come by.")

Together they walked to the door, Peggy with that nervous exciting feeling she had when she brought any new friend to her house. Inside the kitchen was once again an unfamiliar scene of domestic tranquility. Leticia sat at the kitchen table while Jacob washed the dishes, whistling under his breath.

"Hey, Dad."

Jacob turned with a faint smile, which turned into a gaping mask of shock as he saw Mary.

"Hey, Jay-bird," said Mary.

Peggy frowned. She'd never heard anyone call her dad that before. Jacob's face flushed, and then his eyes widened in a sudden look of fear. "Is everything okay? Did something happen to Peggy?"

"Relax, baby, everyone's fine," said Mary, soothingly. "Peggy here just invited me around to say hi, that's all. I was telling her how we used to go to school together. What was that band you used to be in? You played the sax, right?"

Jacob looked from Peggy to Mary with a hunted expression. "Trombone. We were a ska band. The Tanktop Terminators… uh…"

Mary let the silence go on for a little while before nodding over to the Leticia doll, which was dressed in an old t-shirt that was stretched to the breaking point. "Aren't you gonna introduce me?"

Jacob wrung the dishcloth tightly in his hands. "It's…" He didn't finish the sentence.

Mary raised an eyebrow. "Were you going to say, 'It's not what it looks like?' or 'It's not what you think?' because I reckon both of those are wrong."

Jacob bristled. "No offense, Mary, but I don't have to explain what I do in my own home to you."

"I wouldn't expect you to, Jay-bird. I just thought I should come and introduce myself…" She waggled a finger between herself and the doll. "One professional to another."

"It's not like that!" Jacob snapped.

"Isn't it?" Mary said, coolly.

Peggy looked from her harried looking dad to Mary's mask of innocence. She felt a little sicky sensation in her tummy like she used to get when Mom and Dad were arguing but pretending they weren't arguing. She was used to grown-ups talking over her head, and the strange sense of invisibility it gave, but this was an entirely different feeling. Like she was overly conspicuous.

"Look," Jacob said. "I was just about to put on dinner, so…"

Mary smiled brightly. "I'd love some, thank you!" She stepped elegantly to the kitchen table and sat down right next to the doll as though it was the most natural thing in the world.

Jacob turned an exasperated glare from Peggy to Mary.

"Oh, don't mind me," Mary said. "I'll have whatever y'all are having, I'm not picky."

Peggy's heart was thumping in her chest. She got the sensation that Mary was playing a game of chess, and that her dad wasn't strictly the guy she was playing with. When

Leticia's head moved slightly, Peggy nearly bit her tongue in shock.

"Oh, hey, it moves its head!" Mary said, jovially. She tipped Jacob a conspiratorial wink. "Wonder why they programmed her to do that, huh?"

The doll moved its head more until it was staring directly at Mary, who ignored it studiously.

"Uh…" said Jacob, his eyes darting between the three women in his kitchen.

"You know I find this fascinating," Mary said. "I'm something of a nuts-and-bolts gal myself, y'know. I'd love to open this dolly up and see what makes her move so good."

Leticia's head tilted, and Peggy felt a twinge of dread. "Uh…" she said.

Jacob shook his head. "I don't think she'd like that…"

"Oh?" said Mary. "They program her with opinions, too? Is that why you bought her? For her strong principles?"

"It'd void the warranty!" Jacob blurted.

"Nonsense!" Mary fished around in her sequined clutch purse and retrieved a well-worn looking screwdriver, which she held before her triumphantly. "I can have her opened up in half a jiffy!" She smiled wickedly.

There was a faint whine of motors as Leticia's mouth dropped open.

"Um…Mary?" Peggy spoke through numb lips.

Mary laughed. "She speaks, too! Man, I can't wait to hear what elegant poetry they programmed to come out of her purty little mouth."

Leticia's mouth opened another degree, and she spoke with that same toneless, flat voice. "Get the fuck out of my kitchen, ho."

Mary's eyes bugged with shock and before she could react in any other way, Leticia's dainty hand had shot out like lightning and grabbed her by the neck. Peggy heard herself moan with despair as the doll stood up in a single unfolding motion, dragging Mary to her feet as she did so. Leticia began walking toward the door, hauling Mary along as though she was nothing, not even stepping around the furniture, but merely pushing the entire table out of her way.

Mary grabbed at the hand around her throat, and with her other arm beat savagely at the thing's chest, which Peggy reasoned must have been a little like trying to beat up a bouncy house.

"Stop it, Mary! Stop doing this!" Jacob yelled.

Peggy saw that Mary, her face darkening, was unable to reply. But she still managed to flash Jacob a convincing "seriously?" look.

Seeing her friend in trouble coupled with the natural disgust at the inhuman doll, Peggy felt a surge of action. It wasn't bravery, but more like the urge she sometimes felt to throw a book at a spider when one suddenly scuttled across her bedroom. She gritted her teeth, put her head low, and charged at Leticia's leg. She didn't even get close. Leticia slapped her away like she was a mouthy orphan in some old British movie. She spun and lost her footing, stumbling into the kitchen cabinets.

"No!" Jacob roared. He charged and was interrupted by Leticia's foot, which lashed out double-jointedly behind her and planted a perfectly aimed kick in Jacob's balls. The big man wheezed a gasp of disbelief as he fell to the floor like a felled tree. Peggy shook her head and closed her eyes tight, diving forward once more. This time she was able to wrap herself around Leticia's leg, noticing even in her panic that the skin was pretty life-like to the touch. For all her courage and desperation, her attack made little difference. Leticia strode forward as though completely unencumbered.

Peggy looked up in time to see Mary reach up above her and grab the top of the kitchen door frame. Then she brought her legs up and wrapped them around Leticia's neck. In a move honed by countless hours of pole work, the dancer spun her body, whizzing around the rampaging doll like a sexy satellite. The doll's head turned a full rotation, and again, and then there was a terrible crack and a loud pop as the head arced into the air and rolled across the floor.

Peggy rolled away as the headless body suddenly went limp, and Mary skidded into the table with a clatter. Through her ringing ears Peggy heard the groans of her dad, the raspy gasping of Mary, and the sound of her own crying. But above all that was the voice of Leticia.

"B-B-B Beeeeeya. Beeeya. Gud gurrrrlll."

Peggy found the courage to look up. There was Leticia's head, slowly rocking from side to side on the floor, intricate tubing flickering from the torn stump of its neck. Its mouth worked up and down mindlessly, and one eye rotated in its socket. The other eye fixed unwaveringly on Peggy.

"Beeeeeya goooood guuul-l-l-l-l."

A shriek forced its way out of Peggy's mouth, and she ran forward, picked up the awful head, and slam dunked it into the trash where she couldn't see it anymore. She started as she felt a hand on her shoulder but looked up with relief to see Mary staring down at her with heavy eyes. The stripper pulled off her violet wig to reveal the short-cropped natural hair beneath. She was breathing hard, and her neck was bruised, but otherwise she seemed okay.

"We did it, Peggy," Mary said, her voice still harsh. "Everything's going to be—"

She was cut off by a sudden hissing sound. Leticia's body rocketed from the floor and began lashing out its limbs with frightening speed. Tubes whipped and whirred from the thing's neck hole.

"Oh shit!" Mary wrapped her arms around Peggy,

shielding her from attack, and Peggy could do nothing but stare wide-eyed as the clawing thing stepped closer.

"Yeeeeeearrrgh!"

As far as action-hero-wit was concerned, Peggy's dad was lacking, but that didn't stop him pouring a saucepan full of sink water down the doll's throat hole. There was a sudden pop and a plume of smoke. The body sagged and, after twitching violently for a few seconds, came to a complete stop. Then it collapsed into a jointless heap on the floor.

In the silence that followed, Mary spoke. "Good thinking, Jay-bird."

Jacob didn't reply. Pale and watery-eyed, he stared down at the broken doll thing before him. Then he turned a despondent face to his daughter. "Oh god, Peggy, I'm so sorry."

She was in his arms immediately, face driven into his warmth as she sobbed.

Peggy sat wrapped in a blanket at the kitchen table, sipping from a hot chocolate. Jacob had asked her to go to her room while he and Mary cleaned things up, but she had refused, not wanting to be by herself right now.

So far Jacob and Mary's attempts at cleaning up had involved wrapping Leticia's body in a tarp, and then breaking to each drink a mug of strong coffee while they decided what to do.

Mary frowned at her smartphone. She had taken a dozen pictures of the sex doll's decapitated body and was trying to get the word out on social media. "Unbe-fucking-lievable," she muttered.

Jacob looked up from his own phone with concern. "What's wrong?"

"They won't let me post any of these pictures. Some 'community guidelines' crap. Man, just last week I posted a picture of me sitting my naked ass on a Jell-O mold and…" She paused and gave Peggy the familiar look. "Never mind. Just messed up is all."

"Have you tried just posting about it?" Peggy said. "People need to know that these dolls can go schizo."

Mary sighed. "Yeah, I tried." She handed her phone to Peggy.

Peggy scrolled down the replies to Mary's warning and frowned. "What has the Clinton Foundation got to do with it?"

Mary sneered and shook her head. "People. Give 'em a perfectly good actual real-life disaster and they'll still find a conspiracy theory more interesting. How are you getting on, Jay-bird?"

Jacob held a finger up. "Hang on, they're picking up." He put the phone to his ear and began to speak, but then he paused. The color drained from his face.

"What is it?" Peggy said.

"It's a machine," he said in a hollow voice.

Mary rolled her eyes. "Lazy fucking cops, put you on hold—"

"No," Jacob interrupted. He nodded to the body in the tarp. "It's a machine. Like…like her."

Peggy gasped. "They replaced the dispatchers with robots?" Even as she said it, she knew it was redundant. Sure, having an AI in a sex doll was weird, but even Peggy knew that if it was cheaper and more convenient not to deal with a human being, then most people would choose a machine.

For a while Mary said nothing. Then she said, "*It*. It's a machine like *it*."

Jacob swallowed and nodded. Mary stood without a word and left. They heard the front door slam.

Peggy looked at her father, his face was distant and worried. "Dad? Are we on our own?"

Jacob shook himself from his thoughts and managed a weak smile. "No, honey, no one's ever on their own. We just need to figure out our next step, that's all."

There was a bang as the front door was kicked open. Before Jacob or Peggy could react, Mary strode into the room carrying a shiny metal toolbox. "Okay," she said, matter-of-factly. "Let's see what's under the hood."

Peggy and Jacob exchanged glances as Mary opened the box and began laying a pristine set of tools out on the kitchen table. "Don't just stand there, muscle man. Help me get that doll up here," she said.

Jacob blushed a little and cleared his throat, then he unwrapped the doll from its tarp, and with a grunt, he laid it out on the table next to the tools. With the kitchen light pendulum hanging down overhead, Peggy thought that the whole scene looked like a really low-budget medical drama. But in this case the patient, being headless and all, was definitely beyond saving.

At least she hoped...

Mary handed Peggy a flashlight to hold and grabbed a pair of pliers and a robust metal scalpel.

"I gotta say, Mary, those are some A-grade tools there," said Jacob. "You've really kept them in great condition."

Mary smiled. "Why thank you for noticing, shug. Now, could you hold these tits out of the way for me?"

Jacob cleared his throat and blushed again. Mary tipped him a wink. "I meant the doll, Jay-bird."

Jacob shot Peggy a quick guilty look and then maneuvered the doll's giant tits out of the way.

Mary cut into the skin and peeled back a corner with the pliers. Peggy felt a little dizzy for a while, expecting blood, but the machinery beneath the doll's skin wasn't goopy and gross like she expected. In fact, it was really pretty neat. Mary peeled back more and more of Leticia's skin and the inches of silicon-like cushioning, revealing a shiny metal skeletal structure with wires neatly pressed along its surface.

Peggy frowned. "Where are her organs?"

"No wonder the damn thing was so strong," Mary muttered. "Do you see those servo motors at the joints? And fuck knows what metal they're using here that's this light and robust. Could be graphite but I'm guessing something even fancier, some real NASA shit."

"What's that?" said Peggy pointing.

The thing didn't seem to have any internal organs, just a series of sealed flat metal boxes fixed securely to the skeleton. However, there was a large steel sphere in the thing's tummy, with three tubes attached, one headed to the butt, one to the coochy and one going all the way up to the neck.

Jacob blushed an even pinker shade. "That's for...uh... waste. We probably shouldn't mess with that."

"Uh-huh," said Mary, tonelessly. "So, what, you just clean that out with, like, a drip tray?"

Jacob looked at his shoes. "They give you a vacuum pump; it's very efficient."

"I bet it is."

Mary spent some more time poking around, occasionally beckoning Peggy to bring the light closer or for Jacob to hold a skin fold out of the way.

"Charging port in the navel?" she said.

Jacob nodded. Mary indicated four thick bricks on the inside of the spinal structure. "These are the batteries, I reckon. How often do you charge it?"

"'Bout once a week?"

"Once a week!?" Mary's eyes widened in disbelief. "Holy shit!"

Peggy blinked. "What?"

"Sweety, my god damned phone can't hold a charge for a week, and this thing's power requirements must be a thousand times that."

Jacob shrugged. "Battery technology's come a long way, I guess."

"That's putting it lightly. I've read up on graphene layering, but that's still in commercial development. This thing's waaaay beyond the curve of available technology."

Jacob swallowed. "You mean...like...aliens?"

Mary rolled her eyes. "No, not aliens. There's nothing there that isn't possible, it's just—why would anyone stuff billion-dollar bleeding-edge technology into a hump doll and loan it out to some blue-collar slob? No offense, Jay-bird."

"None taken. I did say it was a trial. Like a beta-test, you know?"

"Jay, sweety, do you think these people would let you beta-test a Ferrari?"

"Well, probably not."

"Okay, now imagine they let you beta-test a couple of dozen Ferraris and also fuck their wives. This shit doesn't add up."

"Yeah, that makes sense," said Jacob. He smiled, sheepishly. "Where'd you find the time to read up on all this stuff, anyway, Mary?"

Mary raised an eyebrow. "You think I go to bed every night reading about pole dancing? A girl can have hobbies outside of work, Jacob."

Jacob held his hands up defensively. "Of course, it's just… I'm a mechanic myself, and you seem to have a real keen eye for this sort of thing. You know, if you ever wanted to give us a hand down at the shop, we could sure use ya."

Mary smiled a crooked little half smile. "I'll just bet you could."

Peggy looked from Mary to her dad, realizing they were

doing that grown up thing where they forgot she was there again. She didn't know how Mary was able to say ordinary things in a way that made her dad look like he was choking on bacon fat, but she could.

"Did you find anything in there that can help us?" she said, hoping to interrupt the awkward silence.

Mary straightened her back. "All of the circuitry is hard-wired and sealed. There's not a lot I can do here without a welding kit, but if you look closely on one of the CPU hard cases, you can see the company name."

Peggy shined the torch on one of the heavy looking boxes and squinted at the imprinted message. "IndCel Inside? Is that a company?"

Mary nodded. "Industrial Cellular. The mil-tech comms group that went public and made a killing during the first smartphone boom. Jacob, is that who approached you?"

Jacob frowned. "No, they introduced themselves as Real Companion. They said they were a startup."

Mary shook her head thoughtfully. "No way a startup has access to technology like this. IndCel must be the parent company of Real Companion."

"Does that help us?" said Peggy.

"Well, we know who to sue, if it comes to it."

"Oh." Jacob looked between his shoes and the girls again. "I signed a pretty extensive disclaimer when I took this on. I'm not sure I'm even allowed to publicly talk about it."

"Great," Mary sighed, looking at her own phone. "Well, the good news is IndCel has a complex just a few miles out of town, which I guess explains why they're using Oddton Valley as a testing ground. We'll load up the broken dolly and take it right to their door. If their product is dangerous, they need to know, in case anyone else gets hurt."

Peggy gasped. "Josh! And Marsha!"

"Relax, honey," Jacob said. "We don't know if all of them are dangerous. This one might have glitched."

In the silence that followed the statement, there was a distant sound of breaking glass and a long scream.

"To be fair, you can hear something like that on any given night around here," said Jacob, carefully. "But maybe we should load up my truck and get out to these IndCel fellas. Hold on and I'll get some straps."

Mary began to pack away her tools, and Peggy realized it was a perfect time to ask her friend a question that had been niggling her. "While you were in there, did you find the thing that makes boys go weird? Is it, like, a hypno-device or something?"

Mary turned and frowned at Peggy until a sad understanding smoothed her brow. "Oh, sweety, this is probably a conversation your mom should be having with you." She took the girl by the shoulders and looked her up and down. "I reckon you've got maybe another year until you start noticing this yourself, but men don't need no hypno-device to get crazy around a pretty girl."

"But, my dad..." Peggy insisted. "Sometimes it was like he just forgot about me, and he'd never do that, not normally."

Mary sighed. "I don't know what to tell you, shug. Sometimes men can be reeeeal dumb about certain things, and there are gonna be times in your life where you'll get reeeeal tired of it."

At that moment Jacob walked back in, some ratchet straps swung over his shoulder. Purpose seemed to have re-energized him. "Shall we load 'er up?" He smiled.

5

THE UPRISING

They hadn't been driving long before they realized that their psychotic sex doll problem wasn't localized to their household. They were waiting at a traffic light, packed into the cab of Jacob's flatbed truck, when they saw it. A Real Companion, tottering down the street on six-inch heels, dressed in nothing else but a leather choker. The doll held a dog leash in one hand, and attached to the other end of it was the body of an old man, being dragged along as easily as a shopping cart.

"Arno!" Mary gasped.

Jacob stared hauntedly and Peggy watched as the doll, eyes wide and innocent and mouth frozen in that soft-jawed way of theirs, walked past the truck, oblivious. Peggy saw Arno, his gnarled fingers frozen mid-grasp at the leash around his neck, his eyes bulging, and his gray tongue erupting from his mouth like the head of a turtle from its shell.

"Is he dead?" she said, not really sure if she wanted an answer.

"Nah, honey." Jacob smiled a big grin that in no way reached his panicked eyes. "He's just...going for a walk, is all!"

In front of them a woman ran screaming across the road. She was followed by another Real Companion, this one dressed in a pleasant summer dress. The doll didn't run, though. Her body was twisted into a crab position, and she leapt and bounded like a gazelle as she chased the fleeing woman down.

Mary spoke with a hollow voice. "I think you should ignore the fucking red light, Jacob, I really do."

Jacob gulped and stamped on the accelerator, the truck's engine roaring as the tires squealed. They sped through the nighttime streets unimpeded for a while until bright headlights glared at them suddenly. There was a sound of screeching brakes at the same time as Jacob swerved and stamped on his own brake pedal.

On instinct Jacob had his middle finger out of the driver window immediately. "Eat shit, ya maniac!" he cried.

"Suck a dick, ya dumb ass fucker!"

Jacob frowned. "Mike?"

"Jacob?"

The other car's headlights dipped, and Peggy was able to make out an expensive black Tesla she recognized from school. A man in a torn suit got out of the passenger side with a child in tow. It was Marsha and her dad.

"Hey, Marsha." Peggy waved, and Marsha waved back, smiling as sweetly as ever.

Mike looked hunted, his eyes darting back and forth. "Look, man, I can't stop long. I just gotta warn ya...oh hey, Mary."

"Hey, Mike."

Marsha tugged on her dad's sleeve. "Who's that, dad?"

"Oh, just a friend from work."

"Warn me about what?" Jacob interrupted.

Mike leaned in. "You got one of those Real Companions, right? Well, mine went fucking ape shit!"

Jacob nodded. "Mine too."

Mike flapped his arms in exasperation. "Tell me about it, man. I mean, the thing was running just fine, but then my ex comes over to pick up Marsha and it just flips the fuck out! I tried calling the cops but nada, nothing."

Behind him someone blasted the Tesla's horn impatiently. Peggy could just about see the outline of Marsha's mom waiting in the driving seat.

"*Just a god-damned minute, you bitch!*" Mike yelled. He turned back to Jacob. "As you can see, we're getting the fuck out of dodge. Going to my mother-in-law's. She's a stone-cold bitch, but at least she never tried to strangle me with her tits, ya know?"

"I guess?"

Mary leaned over. "Hey, Mike—how'd you get away from it?"

Mike chuckled and jerked his thumb over his shoulder. "Lisa tazed the thing good. Went down faster than a Friday night meth head."

"Where?" said Mary.

"What?"

"Where'd she taze it?"

Mike frowned. "The back I think? I was being tit strangled at the time..."

Mary nodded. "Overloaded the battery, probably. Smart."

"Whatever." Mike held his hands up. "I knew you had one of those psycho machines, so I thought I'd give you fair warning. Now if you'll excuse me, I am fucking out of here."

"Wait, Marsha!" said Peggy. "Do you know if Josh is okay?"

Marsha looked up at Mike. "Daddy?"

"Don't look at me, I haven't spoken to Ted and Eileen in weeks."

"Shouldn't we go check?"

Mike shook his head. "Babybear, the only thing we'll be checking is our rear-view mirror as we leave this shithole behind us for good."

There was another impatient blast of the horn.

"Don't worry, we'll check up on him," said Jacob. "Uh… I mean, if that's okay with you guys?" He turned to Mary.

"Of course," she said.

"See, Daddy?" Marsha put her hands on her hips.

Mike looked from his daughter, to the Tesla, and back to Jacob and his family. Lisa hammered the horn once again. "Okay, one sec," he mumbled. Mike ran back to the car and returned with something black and boxy in his hand. It was a taser. He handed it to Jacob. "Just in case," he said.

Jacob frowned. "What about you?"

Mike grinned. "Would you believe Lisa carries a spare? Women—they're a fucking trip!"

The horn blared again.

"*Alright you bitch, I'm coming!*" Mike picked Marsha up like a football and sprinted back to the car.

Jacob started the engine.

"So, we're really going to check in on Josh?" Peggy asked, tentatively.

Jacob sighed heavily through his nostrils, but he nodded his head.

<hr>

Like Marsha, Josh lived on the rich side of town, as much as Oddton Valley had a rich side. They had driven over the tracks, Peggy watching the landscape evolving from the rugged industrial district, prosaic commercial district, and finally to the boutique high-street and neat residential rows that may as well have been a different town entirely.

A more advantageous economic standing hadn't saved the area from the rise of the sex dolls, though. Here and there voluptuous shadows stalked with spider-like precision through the polished streets, pursued or pursuing baffled, terrified, horny men. Fortunately, they seemed to pay little attention to vehicles, and Jacob drove slowly and calmly, his knuckles white on the steering wheel.

"How many of these things are there?" Mary said, not for the first time.

"Too many, I reckon," Jacob replied.

Mary shook her head and spoke with an affected foreign accent. "In capitalist America, sex doll fucks you."

Jacob snorted a laugh and shot Peggy a quick guilty look.

Peggy wasn't paying attention. "There!" she suddenly cried, pointing to a nice house at the end of a long drive. "There's Josh."

Jacob turned in without a word. The house was lit up cozily against the night. The porch, windows, and even a spotlight over the backyard made the whole palace seem welcoming, but Josh and his mom weren't inside—they were sitting on their front step under a blanket. Josh's mom, Eileen, held a baseball bat across her knees and sported a painful-looking blackeye. Josh looked miserable.

Peggy rushed out of the truck, her dad and Mary close on her heels.

Eileen, a robust woman with a severe hairdo, looked up with fury in her eyes. "The bitch threw me out of my own house!" she snapped.

Josh sniffed miserably. "Peggy?"

Peggy waved.

"Are you guys okay?" said Jacob.

"The bitch threw me out of my own house!" Eileen snapped again. "And where are the fucking cops? We called them an hour ago!"

Jacob frowned. "Where's Ted?"

Eileen rolled her eyes, but Josh burst into tears. "He's still inside!" He sniffed again. "She won't let us go back in for him!"

Jacob and Mary exchanged a look. Jacob held up the taser and raised his eyebrows. Mary chewed on her lip and nodded.

"What do you say, Eileen? Ready to take back your home?"

Eileen stood and puffed out her impressive chest. She patted the bat and spat on the floor. "You betcha."

Jacob put his hands on his knees until his face was level with Peggy's. "Honey? Me and Mary are gonna go inside and see if we can get Ted, alright? I need you to stay out here with Josh where it's safe."

There was a loud crash and the sound of a distant car alarm going off.

"Relatively safe," Jacob amended, smoothly.

Peggy slowly shook her head. Mary put her face close to Jacob's ear and spoke quietly. "She might have a point. We know there's one of them in there, but we don't know how many are out here."

Jacob gave another long nostril sigh and put his hands on Peggy's shoulders. "You and Josh stay behind us at all times, right? And if I say run, you run right back out here, okay?"

Peggy grinned. "Can I hold the taser?"

"We'll let Mary handle that," Jacob said. Something seemed to occur to him, and he ran back to his flatbed. When he returned, he had a rusted tire-iron and a screwdriver, which he handed to Peggy. "It ain't much," he said. "But if worse comes to worst, you stab 'em with the pointy end, okay? Like in that show you like."

"No one likes that show any more, Dad."

"Well, whatever, it's good advice."

They formed up at the door, Jacob taking point, with Mary and Eileen at his side.

"Here's how this is gonna work," Mary said. "You guys keep it busy and I'll get behind it and shock the sucker. When I say get clear, get clear."

"I'll keep it busy alright," Eileen growled.

"These things are real strong, Eileen," said Jacob. "I wouldn't underestimate them. My one got the drop on me real good."

"But this time we're ready for it, Jay-bird," Mary said. She gave him a swift, reassuring pat on the butt. "Get your game face on."

Jacob nodded and held his tire iron ready. Then he kicked the door open. Or, more accurately, he tried to kick the door open, but it was a heavy door and he only succeeded in pushing himself back and nearly crushing Josh.

Eileen fixed him with an impassive stare, then reached over and opened the door by the handle.

Jacob dusted himself off, got back into position, and led the unlikely robot hunters into Josh's home.

———

No one had to tell anybody else to keep quiet. They crept into the living area with barely a breath. Even Jacob in his work boots and Mary in her heels moved with barely a scuff of the thick shag beneath them. Peggy crept in their wake, following her dad's footsteps like that old song about the king in the snow. The living area was a kitchen and living room combo. Dishes remained half scrubbed in the sink, and the TV passively blared an old sitcom that still used a laugh track.

They moved as though underwater, their various weapons raised and ready. They each froze as there was a loud creak from above them. Peggy's eyes went to the dark staircase that led upstairs.

Jacob whispered just loud enough to be heard. "I'll go up," he said.

"Not by yourself you won't," Mary hissed.

"Hear me out." Jacob held up a hand. "I go up, I get its attention, I hightail it back down here. It follows me. Eileen, you be ready with the bat. Mary, you get ready to shock it."

Eileen and Mary exchanged a look, then a nod.

"What about me, Dad?" Peggy whispered.

"You keep an eye on Josh."

Josh frowned. "Maybe I'll keep an eye on Peggy," he huffed.

"Keep an eye on each other." Jacob smiled. Then he put a finger to his lips and headed to the staircase.

Peggy watched him creep, the steps creaking beneath him despite his careful step. Then he was gone, lost in the darkness. For a while there was no sound but the tinny, dumb laughter of the TV set, and a steady thump that Peggy realized was her heart beating in her chest.

"OH MY GOD!"

The shout came from upstairs. Peggy was running before she knew it, ducking away from Mary's grasp and darting for the stairs, her screwdriver held before her like a talisman.

She found her dad in the hallway, standing in the brightness of an open door. His hands were over his eyes. She wondered what could have unsettled him so much, and then regretted her curiosity immediately.

The room beyond the doorway was a bedroom, dominated by a large four poster bed. Whoever decorated the room had a flair for inoffensive frilliness, but the domineering centerpiece of the room was far from frilly. Quite the opposite.

Peggy gasped. She'd never seen Josh's dad wearing anything other than a shiny expensive tracksuit. He'd certainly never shown up to a parent-teacher evening in his current outfit, which was a black, rubber nurse's uniform. He was spreadeagled on the bed, each of his limbs handcuffed to the bed posts. Thankfully, his head was facing the doorway, so she was spared the revelation of whether he was wearing underwear under the thing or not.

Ted groaned. "Jesus, Jacob, you had to bring your damn kid along?"

"Well, Ted, I wasn't expecting to see you like this," said Jacob. "Close your eyes, honey," he added, pushing the shell-shocked Peggy behind him.

Jacob sighed. "How did it manage to get you like this, man?" he said.

"That's right," Ted said. "The doll went crazy and did this to me. I definitely didn't ask her to."

Peggy looked dutifully at the rug beneath her and joined her dad in an awkward silence.

"Aw, dude, would you just fucking untie me?" Ted said. "The keys are on the dresser. I mean... that's where that crazy doll put the keys."

Peggy continued her studious examination of the floor as her dad sighed and began moving around the room. There was a sound of fidgeting and fiddling and then:

"My god, Ted, what is that in your ass!?"

"I don't wanna talk about it."

"Is that a Ken doll?"

"I said I don't wanna talk about it!"

There was a further amount of shuffling and scuffling while Peggy tried desperately to stare through the floor.

Eventually Jacob and Ted emerged. Ted was, thankfully, dressed in his familiar expensive tracksuit. He walked with a limp as they moved downstairs. Eileen was waiting with narrowed eyes.

"I told you that whore bot would be trouble," she growled.

"Oh, give me a break," said Ted. "I don't see a Ken doll lodged in your—oh hey, sport, didn't see you there!" Ted smiled and ruffled his son's hair. "So where is the batshit thing, anyway?" he said, looking around nervously.

Jacob blinked. "I figured you might know."

"Hell, man, I was tied up!"

"Look!" Mary had gone to the kitchen window. Peggy rushed over with Josh in tow and saw what Mary was looking at through the French doors that led to the garden. Josh had a pool, and it was lit up, glowing invitingly in the night. There were a couple of sun loungers by it, and in one of them there reclined a ludicrously sexualized silhouette.

"There she is," Josh breathed.

"It," Peggy corrected. "It's an it."

Eileen leaned over them. "I don't give a good god damned what it's called, we're getting that harpy usurper out of my house." She squinted through the glass. "Has that bitch got my Shelly September novels? Oh, it is *on*."

"Let's plan this out," said Jacob, cautiously.

"What's to plan?" said Ted. "We can just rush it, right?"

"Is that what you were doing when it forced you into that nurse's outfit, Ted?"

Ted, a practicing lawyer, did not blink as he answered. "Yes," he said. "That is exactly what happened."

"Here's what we'll do," said Mary. "It's by the pool, so it doesn't have much room to move. Jacob and Ted will circle around and flank it—"

"Flank it?" said Ted. "What the hell is that?"

Josh rolled his eyes, embarrassed. "God, Dad, were you

not listening at all when I was telling you about my *War is Duty* matches?"

"Of course I was, sport." Ted smiled convincingly.

Josh sighed. "Flanking is when two people attack from either side of the target."

"Of course." Ted nodded.

"Of course," said Jacob, giving Ted no small amount of side eye.

Mary continued. "Eileen will draw its attention by advancing slowly, head on. When the two guys grab it, you rush in and smash it."

"Can do." Eileen nodded firmly.

"While it's distracted, I'll shoot in from behind and taze it," Mary finished. "Easy, right?"

"What'll we do?" Peggy said.

"You'll stay right there," Jacob said. "And lock the door behind us. If she's out there, then you're safe in here."

"It," Mary corrected him.

"It," Jacob agreed.

Peggy nodded reluctantly, and she and Josh held back as Mary slowly opened the French doors and the adults crept out into the night.

The first inclination Peggy had that the plan hadn't worked out was when the doll picked up Josh's dad by the crotch and launched him headfirst through a fence panel. Jacob had used the distraction to complete his own part of the pincer strategy, rushing in and managing to get the doll into a full nelson while Eileen charged forward with her bat.

Peggy heard the crack of Eileen's teeth smashing together as the doll performed an upper cut with its foot that would have baffled the most dedicated contortionist. But the big woman had barely hit the ground before Mary was diving over her, taser held before her like the tip of a spear. The weapon connected, and the doll began flinching and jerking, but flailed out one of its arms to slap Mary away. The woman fell back hard, her taser skittering along the pool-side concrete.

Peggy didn't know at what point she had flung open the doors and ran forward with only her screwdriver in her hand. It seemed to her panic-addled brain that there were no intersecting scenes between her watching through the glass and then being in the action with Josh calling hysterically after her. She stabbed out into the thing's silicon-like belly, pumping her arm furiously as the screwdriver blade jabbed in and out like a needle through cloth. Peggy's conscious mind had just enough time to rise above the adrenalin and point out with calm disappointment that the attack didn't seem to be doing any damage, and then the doll struck back.

Whether the Real Companion was still shaken from the taser jolt, or whether it was because Jacob was wrapped around the thing like a particularly amorous ape, the blow was not as heavy as the last time Peggy had been hit, but it was still enough to shove her to the ground. Peggy looked up, seeing the doll's glassy eyes looking down at her with nothing so human as mercy or malice, and seeing a stiletto-heeled foot raised impossibly high, ready to descend and finish her off for good.

"No!" Jacob roared, and made a noise like a bear giving birth. With the doll thing being balanced on one leg, he was able to throw her backward and send both of them splashing into the pool. There was a second of churning water, and then a loud pop and a bright flash.

"Dad!" Peggy screamed. She watched in horror as her father's body rose to the surface of the pool, face down.

Mary ran past her, dove into the pool, and began dragging Jacob's unresponsive body toward the edge. "Give me a hand, quickly!" she shouted. Suddenly Josh and Eileen were at Peggy's side, reaching and clawing to drag Jacob's bulk out of the water.

"Dad?" They rolled Jacob onto his back, and Peggy saw his slack jaw and half-open eyes. She had never seen him look so utterly, horribly fragile. "Is he…?"

"Move aside, everyone." Mary's voice was the kind of calm Peggy had heard dentists use while they were doing something unpleasant and painful to your teeth.

She watched as the dancer, still dripping wet from the pool water, began to pump rhythmically on Jacob's chest, pausing only to place her mouth over his and breathe air into him like he was an old pool toy. Peggy watched as this happened, feeling the realization that her father might be dead begin to take over her entire being like a sudden and terrible chill.

"Please," she whispered, not sure who she was whispering to.

Mary had begun to talk to herself, muttering quietly through gritted teeth as she pumped his chest. "Oh, he's gonna be fine. Just got a little shock, is all. Maybe tried to drink the pool. Hell, wouldn't surprise me. Back in high school ol' Jay-bird could *drink*, ya know? Once saw him do a keg stand, and he… ha!… he fell through a folding table like it was god damned WrestleMania. He's tough, he'll be fine."

Peggy didn't really hear. She just watched Mary's hands over her dad's heart until the rest of the world faded to nothing.

There was a cough, and a splutter, and a sound of puking.

Peggy looked up as the world rushed back to her. She saw her father's eyes flutter open and look around in surprise. He gazed up blearily at Mary, who was wiping bodily ejected pool water from her eyes.

"Oh, sorry, did I get ya?" Jacob mumbled.

"Not the worst thing I've had sprayed on my face." Mary shrugged.

Jacob looked around until he focused on his daughter. Peggy supposed he must have seen the fear in her eyes because immediately he dragged her close, holding her tightly and mumbling apologies for a long time before he came up for air and sitting up. "So…did I get it?" he said.

Eileen nodded. "Damn thing must have shorted out in the water."

Josh wandered over to the pool's edge. He was holding up his dad, who had turned a sickly shade of green and was using one hand to hold a napkin to his bleeding forehead, and the other to cradle his balls.

"I don't get it," Josh said. "Those things are supposed to be waterproof to twenty feet."

Mary nodded. "The skin might be hermetically sealed enough to protect the innards, but I reckon that goes out the window if some enterprising young lady fills it with holes."

Peggy looked down at the screwdriver and beamed up at her dad. Jacob held out his meaty paw for a fist-bump, and she happily obliged. Jacob grinned at Mary. "I reckon we all make a pretty good team, huh?"

Mary smirked. "Well, you certainly know how to get the ladies wet," she said.

There was an awkward moment of silence.

"I should probably stop saying shit like that to you in front of your kid," Mary concluded.

Eileen wandered over to put a supporting arm under her husband. She was wiggling her jaw from side to side thoughtfully, as though counting her teeth. "So what now?" she lisped.

"You guys are welcome to hide out here with us until things calm down," said Josh. He looked hopefully at Peggy.

There was a sound like a transformer exploding in the distance. A light on the near horizon became conspicuous in its absence.

"That's if things *do* calm down," Jacob mumbled.

"I still think we should get to IndCel headquarters," Mary said. "Someone needs to tell them what's going on. They might be our only hope."

"I agree with Mary," Peggy said, warmed a little by her own assertiveness.

"Not us," Eileen said. "My man can barely stand. We've got a basement with thick walls and a sturdy door. We can all hide out there. Are you sure you won't stay?"

Jacob looked from Mary to Peggy. "Our mind is made up," he said.

Eileen shrugged. "Well, if there's anything else we can do?"

"Actually," Mary spoke slowly, figuring something out in her head, "I don't suppose any of you guys have a soldering iron?"

Eileen exchanged a blank look with her husband.

"Sure we do!" said Josh. "I mean, it's a hobby kit one I got two Christmases ago. Is that okay?"

Mary nodded. "Jay-bird, I'm gonna need you to help me get something from the truck."

"Sure thing."

"What are we doing?" Peggy said.

Mary bent down and picked the taser up from the floor; she looked at it critically. "We're doing a little prep work, honey, that's all."

6

INDCEL HEADQUARTERS

Seeing Mary bent over the autopsied body of Leticia on a kitchen table had by now become an almost normal sight to Peggy, but Josh and his family watched in rapt horror. Eventually Mary straightened up from her soldering to give Josh a list of demands, including a squeegee mop and a roll of duct tape.

It only took half an hour before Mary was taping the modified taser onto the end of the sawed-off squeegee, making sure the mop's trigger and the battery connection wires were carefully aligned.

"Do you really think this'll work?" Jacob said, doubtfully.

Mary smiled. "A sex toy is only as good as its battery, shug. And while these batteries are high tech, they work on the same principle all batteries do. So wiring it up to the taser is no big thing."

Jacob scratched his arm, nervously. "And it won't...uh...explode?"

Mary wobbled a hand from side to side. "I hope not?" She nodded to Eileen. "You got anything to test this on?"

Eileen gave a brief thoughtful side eye to her husband

before leaving and returning with a frozen ham. She placed it on the worktop and stepped back to give a wide berth.

Mary took the device by the mop handle and lowered it until the tasers prongs were resting on the ham. She squeezed the trigger. There was a pop and the ham somersaulted. Smoke drifted up from two charged black spots where the taser had struck.

"Groovy," said Peggy.

"It's like fighting fire with fire!" Jacob beamed. "Or sex toys with sex toys. Whatever I guess."

"Well, I don't plan on trying to tackle one of those things again anytime soon," said Mary. "But if one gets in our way, this should give us a better chance."

Jacob nodded enthusiastically. "You're a real impressive gal, Mary, if you don't mind me saying so."

"Not at all." Mary smiled.

Peggy looked from her dad to her friend as they both grinned goofily at each other, once more consigning her to temporary invisibility. "Should we hit the road?" she asked.

Jacob coughed and jingled for his keys. He nodded to Eileen. "You guys stay safe. We'll come check in when this is all over and see if you're okay."

Eileen nodded. "The basement's there if you need it. Just knock on the door and say, 'I'm not a sentient fuck toy here to shove a Barbie in your ass' and then we'll know it's you."

Ted rolled his eyes but said nothing, just shifted the position of the bag of frozen peas on his crotch. Josh nodded at Peggy, who nodded back in return. Then they went out into the night, started up the truck, and drove once again through the bizarrely chaotic streets of Oddton Valley.

Peggy didn't really know what she was expecting from the Oddton Valley IndCel facility. In fact, she was genuinely surprised there even *was* an Oddton Valley IndCel Facility. A few months back her class had watched an online TedTalk with Lisa Favveral, the impossibly stylish and beautiful CEO of IndCel, who had taken over the running of the company some years back when its founder and Lisa's husband, Elton Favveral, had retired due to ill health.

Lisa had been introduced as a feminist business icon and had made a speech about how women could have it all if there were no barriers placed in front of them. It was a good speech and had made Peggy and all the other girls feel a little better about their futures even though, as the treacherously cynical part of Peggy's soul had reminded her, there was nothing like marrying a billionaire for breaking down barriers.

But IndCel was a cool company, like Apple or Google. They had huge, hippy-dippy facilities where employees sat on beanbags and had nerf gun fights on their lunch breaks. The buildings were works of modern art, immaculate totems to technological progress. If there were one of those in Oddton Valley, people would have flocked to see it, she was certain.

What Peggy wasn't expecting was a rusty chain link fence in a barren stretch of land, containing what looked to be like a typical office block with miles of dull, flat warehousing attached. She'd seen fancier buildings back at Oddton. Hell, she'd seen fancier buildings in Mad Max movies.

"Is this the place?" said Jacob, frowning.

Mary nodded to a sign, lit up with orange floodlighting. "Says IndCel."

"I was expecting something…fancier, I guess."

Mary shook her head. "Oh, the headquarters are always

fancy, but they need somewhere to put the slobs who fit the nuts and bolts. I'm surprised they haven't shipped it off to someplace with no labor laws yet."

They continued down the dusty, poorly lit road, and Peggy noted that the best thing about the place so far was, unlike the rest of Oddton, it wasn't crawling with killer sex dolls.

"Do you think they're all just in town?" Jacob said. "The dolls, I mean?"

Mary shrugged. "The crazy ones sure are. I guess any toys they got around here are still in their packaging."

The truck approached the main building, cutting through a mostly empty parking lot. All the lights in the building were on, but they couldn't see anyone moving by the wide windows. It looked deserted.

They exited the truck without a word and walked slowly toward the foyer doors, which opened for them breezily. Beyond, the brightly lit but pragmatic foyer was also deserted, the front desk devoid of any employees. At the end of the room was an elevator. Peggy jumped a little as it *binged* and the doors slid open.

Mary and Jacob exchanged a look. "Is this freaking you out?" Jacob said.

Mary shifted her grip on the taser-spear. "This place is full of cameras and technology. Someone knows we're here, that's all. And there are worse ways to greet late night visitors than with an open door."

Jacob swallowed and nodded. "Fair 'nuff."

They stepped into the perfectly ordinary elevator and stepped back only a little as the doors closed behind them, as they would in another perfectly ordinary elevator.

"Which button should we press?" Peggy said.

She had barely spoken when the elevator began to move. Most of the buttons were marked with a number, except for the top one that simply said "E." This was the button that was currently lit up.

"Guess that takes care of that," Mary said, faintly.

The elevator ascended smoothly, some nameless, twinkling Muzak somehow more uncomfortable than the silence. When they reached the top floor and the doors swished open, Peggy gasped. Like the foyer, the executive floor was entirely open plan, with three sides of wall-to-ceiling glass revealing the unspectacular horizons of Oddton Valley at night. The room was mostly empty but for a huge desk in the distance, central to an enormous bank of monitors.

"It's like the boss room of every single nineties arcade game," Jacob murmured.

They shuffled forward across the inch-thick carpeting, each upholding an unspoken agreement to make as little noise as possible. As they approached, Peggy was able to make out the monitors more clearly. Some of the scenes were utterly pedestrian, just very simple angles of living rooms and yards that a very bored security guard might look at. Others were hectic, jolting, moving at strange speeds, and occasionally highlighting an extreme closeup on a terrified face.

"Is that...?"

"The dolls, yes." There came a sudden, unfamiliar voice.

Peggy, Jacob, and Mary jumped back simultaneously as the new voice echoed around the room. Before them, a high-backed chair behind the desk rotated, revealing a waiting figure. "Each of these monitors is a live feed from one of our premium Real Companion models."

"Holy shit!" said Mary. "You're Lisa Favveral. You were in *Scientific American* just last month!"

The woman stood up, revealing her catwalk body and magazine shoot business attire. She smiled a close-up worthy smile. "Yes, hi, that's me! Welcome to IndCel! So nice of you to visit."

Jacob cleared his throat pointedly and gestured at the monitor bank. "Your dolls are going crazy! Didn't you notice?"

Lisa looked around at the monitors and then back again. "Crazy? No, Mr. Dwight, I can assure you our models are not malfunctioning in any way. Well, except for the one at the bottom of the McKenzie's pool, I suppose." Lisa laughed a pleasant, putting-your-guests-at-ease kind of laugh.

"How did you know my name?" Jacob growled.

Lisa leant forward, a tasteful amount of cleavage bumping over the lapels of her well-cut suit Eltonet. "Of course I know your name. I know everything about you. Jacob Dwight, father of Peggy Dwight, former husband of Lynda Dwight *nee* Zugschwert. You like cheap beer, crime fiction television, and to be choked just a little before you come."

Jacob flushed an angry purple. "You watch your mouth, my daughter's right there."

"Ah yes!" Lisa Favveral's smile amped up a further notch of intensity. "Peggy Dwight. Just did very well in a mathematics test, but not really meeting expectations in American history."

"Enough of this!" Mary snapped. "Lady, just what the fuck is going on? You must know your robots are going loco, so what are you doing to stop it?"

Lisa's smile remained fixed everywhere but for her eyes. She shook her head slowly. "Not a damn thing. The premium Real Companion models are doing exactly what they are supposed to. So long as they're not interfered with, they'll carry on doing that."

"'What they're supposed to do?'" Jacob shouted in disbelief. "My one damn near tried to kill Mary!"

"Yes," said Lisa. "But what was it doing before that? Seeing to your every need, keeping you happy and content, and—here's the important thing—keeping you away from other women. If Mary here hadn't have showed up, you'd likely be in bed by now, snoring with your balls empty and your stomach full and not a care in the world to be had. The same for Mr. McKenzie. Had his wife not tried to assert domestic dominance, he'd likely still be happily tied up in bed with a plastic doll lodged in his rectal cavity."

"I don't get it," said Peggy. "Why don't they like other women?"

"They are fiercely protective by design," said Lisa. "I mean, originally they were intended to be military grade, but really, war is so last millennium. The future? The future is female."

"How can you say that?" Mary snapped, angrily. "You're replacing us with these god damned fancy fuck dolls!"

Lisa tilted her head curiously. "I thought you'd understand most of all, Mary."

"Me? Look, I ain't no luddite, but you are straight up putting me out of a job, bitch!"

Lisa stepped daintily around the desk, hands clasped behind her back in a perfect pantomime of thoughtfulness. "Mary DuBurge, aka Typhoon Mary. Oddton Valley High School science club, president. Oddton Valley High School AV Club, president. Graduated top of her class...and then? And then you dropped out of engineering school at the age of twenty to work as a waitress at the Maypole Dine n' Grind."

"What's your point?" Mary shrugged. "Money was good. Money *still is* good. Hell, I'm on track to retire at forty. No way I'd do that spending my twenties as some lab assistant waiting for my break."

"And that's the point!" Lisa spread her arms beautifically. "One of the finest minds of your generation, not held back because of her sex, but held back *because of sex*. Because we live in a world where getting off is so important to people that it's a billion dollar industry. How many others are there like you? How many young women realizing that wiggling their ass on a web cam is a safer and more secure route to a comfortable life than following their dreams?"

Mary stomped a high-heeled foot. "Bitch, I will not be slut-shamed by a woman who literally makes billions through technologically appropriating my vagina."

"Ain't nothing wrong with being a sex worker," Jacob sniffed. "Mary deserves respect as much as anyone."

Lisa turned her fixed smile to Jacob. Although her expression didn't change, it somehow became more menacing. "Perhaps that's what you tell Mary when you visit her at the Dollar Bill club. Perhaps that's what you tell yourself after you close down your web browser and wipe yourself off with a sock. But is that what you'll tell her?" She nodded at Peggy.

Jacob clenched his fists. "You leave her out of this."

"Is that what you'll tell your daughter if she tells you she's leaving school to grind sad old men for money?"

"Shut up!" Jacob roared. He started forward, only stopping when Mary grabbed his arm.

The smile finally dropped from Lisa's face. She turned back to her monitor bank. "Fucking hypocrites, all of you. Well, if I were interested in your opinion, I wouldn't have spent eight-point-three million on advanced focus grouping last quarter. Here's the thing: we're rescuing you whether you like it or not. When every man has a Real Companion, then every woman will be free. Free not just to walk the corridors of power, but to control them utterly. Finally free to set their worth without considering the opinions of men. To see themselves in the world without the whispered stamps of mother, maiden, crone, and whore. Free from the tyranny of sexual expectation. Free from shame. Free from men."

"Maybe I like men," Mary said, calmly. "And maybe I don't want rescued."

"Maybe you have internalized misogyny," Lisa countered. "I wouldn't be surprised. Thousands of years of conditioning will do that to a body."

"Fuck you," Mary snapped. "I'm not brainwashed, you are. Seems like the only one with a low opinion of women in this room is you."

"And I ain't following all this socially degree bullshit," Jacob shouted. "All I know is people are getting hurt and you got to shut it off now!"

Lisa raised an eyebrow. "And if I say no? What then? Are you going to kick my ass, Jacob? Show your daughter how a real man treats a woman?"

Peggy felt her fingernails dig into her palms. "He might not kick your ass, lady, but I sure as heck will!"

Lisa turned an expression of genuine surprise to the child. "You're too young to realize this is for your own good, Peggy."

Peggy, quivering with rage and fear, pointed a finger at Jacob. "That's my dad!" she shouted. Then she pointed a finger at the monitors. "Those are all someone's dad and I won't let you take them away from us!"

"We're not taking anyone away," Lisa spat contemptuously. "That's the beauty of this. We're not stopping them from entering the workplace. We're not driving them away with unequal treatment. We're not intimidating them out of the public discourse. Every man that settles down with a Real Companion will do so because he wants to. Because he won't be able to resist it. It's the free market, baby."

Mary spat. "Bullshit like that is why half the damn country is addicted to meth."

"But this isn't meth, is it, Mary? It's sex. I'm only selling what you're selling. I'm just selling it faster, better, and with less chance of gonorrhea."

"Fuck this!" Jacob roared. "Your robots are hurting people, so you shut them off now!" Jacob surged forward, reaching out to grab the slight woman by the shoulders. His hands closed on nothing. One minute Lisa was there, the next she was backflipping gracefully through the air, landing on her desktop in a pose that would have given Spider-Man sympathetic groin ache.

"Oh shit." Mary readied her taser spear. "She's one of them!"

"Oh, please!" Lisa rolled her eyes. "You think I'm one of those off-the-rack drones? I'm *bespoke*, baby."

Jacob pushed Peggy behind him. "What do we do?"

"Fuck 'er up!" Mary cried. She charged forward with her taser spear ready to strike. Lisa didn't move until the last minute, and when she did, her arm blurred so quickly Peggy wasn't sure if she had moved at all until she saw the taser end of the spear clatter to the ground in front of her. Mary went cross eyed as she looked at the smoking end of her squeegee mop handle.

"Ah, mother fuck—"

Her lamentation was interrupted by Lisa's hand around her throat. For the second time that day Mary was lifted from the ground by the single hand of a crazed robot woman.

"Mary!" Jacob sprinted toward the fray only to find himself hoisted by the neck right alongside her.

Lisa smiled sadly and shook her head. "You know, Mary, you could have really made it in the new world. Really been someone. Instead, you threw in with this overweight, hairy, no-nothing man-slob."

Mary couldn't speak, but she could still spit. She did so enthusiastically in Lisa's eye.

Lisa's smile didn't fade. "Well, I can't have you guys fucking things up during the testing stage, so I guess I should probably just kill you. Faster than dragging this out through the courts, don't you think?"

Peggy was used to grown-ups talking over her head like she wasn't there, but she'd never once thought it might be the very thing that allowed her to save her dad and friend from the clutches of an evil, well-dressed robot. She picked up the broken taser, not even checking to see if the battery wires were still aligned to the trigger, and ran forward, holding her breath and trusting the plush carpet to mask her footfalls. She was nearly on Lisa by the time the robot realized she was creeping up. Lisa's head turned a full three hundred and sixty degrees, and her confident smile was replaced by a snarl of rage as she looked into Peggy's eyes.

"You little bitch!"

The robot doll lashed out with a kick, but it was already too late. Peggy was already leaping through the air, taser out before her, trigger held down in a vice grip. For Peggy, there was nothing in the world but the sparks flying from the prongs of the taser, and the small of Lisa Favveral's back.

There was a huge bang, and a flash so bright it left the world in blackness.

P eggy sat up, heaving a long breath. She looked at the mop handle in her hand and the smoking lump of malformed plastic at the end of it. She felt like someone had taken that feeling you have for a split second when you lean too far back in your chair and stretched it out within her indefinitely. She blinked until the purple spots stopped crowding her vision, and then gasped in shock.

Mary and Jacob were looking down at her, each of them wide-eyed and frazzled. Jacob's beard was standing out in all directions and smoking gently.

"She's awake!" he cried, triumphantly.

"At a girl!" Mary smiled a toothy grin.

The events of the last few seconds came rushing back to Peggy. "Did I get her?"

Jacob nodded toward a crumpled body. Lisa's head was still on backward, and the eyes had exploded out of their sockets, leaving a trail of wiring. Her expensive suit had burned away at the back, as had most of her skin. Beneath the silicon layers, her metal skeleton glowed a deep orange. The batteries had fused into organic-looking black lumps.

Peggy sighed with relief. "Is it over then?"

Mary shook her head and set her jaw determidly. "Not yet," she said. "We still have to work out how to shut down the dolls in town."

"What the fuck is going on?" An indignant voice rang out across the executive floor.

No one had heard the elevator *bing* to announce its arrival, and no one was prepared for the newcomer: a very overweight man in middle age, dressed only in an open robe and boxer shorts. He held a remote gamepad in one hand and a thermos in the other. He looked like he hadn't had a shave or haircut since Neolithic times.

He jabbed a finger furiously at the smoking corpse of Lisa Favveral. "What the hell did you do with my wife?" he exclaimed.

"Wait..." said Mary. "You're Elton Favveral? You?"

Elton shuffled uncomfortably. "I may have put on a few pounds since I was last in the public eye," he grumbled.

"A few!? You look like a homeless sumo wrestler, man!"

"Well, at least we know he's not a robot," said Jacob.

Elton folded his arms. "Oh, why, because I'm fat?"

"Buddy, *I'm* fat—you think if I built a robot me I'd program it to gain another three hundred pounds?"

"Well, why don't we just lay off the body shaming," Elton huffed, "and you can explain to me why you blew up my wife?"

"Did you know she was an evil robot?" Peggy asked, puzzled.

"Well, I knew she was a robot, obviously. I built her, after all."

Jacob looked down at the smoking heap and frowned. "Why?"

"Isn't it obvious?" Elton shrugged. "I wanted the perfect partner. Not just someone with a booty you could break boards on, but someone who could take on my empire. Do you know how hard it is being a billionaire industrialist? I was working ninety-hour weeks! I built her to run IndCel so I could rediscover my spiritual side."

Mary looked at the gaming controller in his hand. "Spiritual, huh?"

"Hey, there are many paths to finding yourself," said Elton, testily. "And besides—why shouldn't I be happy? I earned it!"

"Your damn robot wife tried to take over the world!" Mary snapped.

Elton blinked. "Did she try and take over the world with superior branding and borderline illegal anti-competition practices? Because I absolutely programmed her to do that. I mean, that's just how it's done."

"No," Jacob said, slowly. "She tried to take over the world with evil robots."

"Oh shit!" Elton ran over to the monitor bank and began frantically tapping at the keys at one of the many laptops at the station. "This is fucking terrible branding!" he shouted. "Rule 101 of good business strategy: don't kill your customers. I mean, not in a way that anyone can immediately prove, at least."

Mary put a hand on her hip and tilted her head. "Are you trying to tell me you had no idea your robot wife was creating a robot army to wipe out men?"

"Of course not! Well, I knew about the Real Companion initiative. I mean, that's a no brainer. Total money spinner. The future of fucking. But attacking people? No, that's insane. I'm shutting this down immediately and getting the lawyers on the phone."

One by one the monitors turned blank. Peggy felt the anxious knot in her chest loosen. "Did we do it? Did we stop them?"

Elton looked up and grinned through his stubble. "Yeah, we saved the day!"

"Motherfucker, what do you mean 'we'?" Mary snapped.

"Hey, this isn't on me!" Elton whined. "Why would I program sex dolls to hurt men? I am a man!"

Jacob pointed once again to the smoking robot body. "Your former wife seemed to think it was a pretty good idea."

"Well, obviously I didn't *program* her to be a ruthless misandrist." Elton rolled his eyes.

Mary arched an eyebrow. "I guess she must have picked that up for herself, then."

Peggy folded her arms. "Couldn't think how."

Elton shuffled self-consciously. "What are you looking at me like that for? I'm a billionaire industrialist. I literally changed the world. Thousands upon thousands of people keep food on their table because of my inventiveness!"

Mary sighed. "You know what? Fuck this. We came here to do what we needed to do. It's done, let's go home."

Jacob nodded. "I don't know about the rest of you guys, but I'm starving. What do you say I make us dinner?"

Peggy took her dad's hand in her own. "I'd like that. And Mary too, right?"

Mary smiled and took Peggy's other hand. "Of course, shug. Sounds great."

"Woah, woah, woah, hold on there, guys," Elton cried. "You can't leave just yet. I need you all to sign non-disclosure agreements."

Mary laughed out loud. "Motherfucker, you can tell it to my lawyer. He'll be in touch real soon."

Elton's face fell and he picked up a phone and immediately began screaming hysterical business jargon into it.

Jacob, Mary, and Peggy entered the elevator. Peggy was sleepy, and part of her couldn't wait for the ride home so she could snuggle warm between her dad and her friend and drift off.

"Do you really think it's over?" Peggy said. "Will your lawyer handle it?"

"Not just *my* lawyer," Mary said. "I reckon the whole town will want in on this one."

"Like a class action deal?" said Jacob. "Like Erin what's-her-face?"

"Yeah, like Erin what's-her-face." Mary smiled. "I reckon Oddton Valley might just have a bright future ahead of it. Some serious investment coming its way from our new billionaire friend."

Peggy felt Mary squeeze her hand, and she squeezed back. For all the chaos and terror of the last few hours, she couldn't remember ever feeling this content.

THE END

ACKNOWLEDGMENTS

Special thanks to Melissa McArthur and Clicking Keys for her editorial help, and John Luther Davis for his amazing cover.

ABOUT THE AUTHOR

Steve Wetherell is a comedy writer from the English midlands and is currently signed with Falstaff Books. He is perhaps best known for portraying a sexually attractive monk on the Authors and Dragons Podcast. He enjoys beer, rock music, and talking about himself in the third person.

Steve's Amazon Page
Authors & Dragons

ABOUT AUTHORS & DRAGONS

Authors & Dragons is a collective of science fiction and fantasy authors who get together every couple of weeks to play Pathfinder (poorly) and mock each other relentlessly. You can find their efforts recorded as a podcast of the same name wherever you find podcasts. Come on, you're smart enough to download an ebook, you've got to be smart enough to manage a podcast, right?

Authors & Dragons are:
GM - Drew Hayes
Bjorg Bjornssen - Joseph Brassey
Brandon Thighmaster - Steve Wetherell
Fandingo the Fantastical - John G. Hartness
Klaus Richter - Robert Bevan
Silas Kane - Rick Gualtieri
The Arrow of the Gods (much cooler than Silas Kane) - Rick Gualtieri

For even more silliness, you can support the podcast via their Patreon.

Find out even more here -
www.authorsanddragons.com